Forests of Silver, Forests of Gold

Tales of Crones, Maids and Mothers

C.E. COLLINS

Dear Nicola

I hope you enjoy these tales. I get my inspiration always from landscapes (I am the sort of impossible person who weeps at the beauty of early morning - don't recommend, you never get anything done) and my family - our own little coven.

I hope you build your own coven - every woman needs one.

Chris

To my sister and mother,

who inspire all my stories, really.

Forests of Silver, Forests of Gold:

Tales of Crones, Maids and Mothers

by C. E. Collins

Cover design and all illustrations

by Rebecca Freeman

First Published in the UK in 2021 by:

BTS Books,
22 Bramwith Road,
Sheffield,
United Kingdom,
S11 7EZ

ISBN: 978-0-9565251-5-4

Designed and typeset by Between These Shores Books (BTS).

British Cataloguing-in-publication Data: a catalogue record for this book can be obtained from the British Library

Acknowledgement: 'One for Sorrow' was first published by *Enchanted Conversation*, April 2019

Forests of Silver, Forests of Gold

Tales of Crones, Maids and Mothers

by
C. E. Collins

Cover design and all illustrations
by
Rebecca Freeman

A Shorelines Series Collection
From

Between These Shores Books

Forests of Silver, Forests of Gold

One for Sorrow, Two for Joy

'Sly, crafty old magpie,' grandma said. She smiled and we watched wide eyed as she smiled her hundred-times grin; each crease in her face beaming another curve; sideways, upside down.

'They steal you know.' We watched her reach up to the tufts of twigs in the apple tree, blinded by the sun. We ducked from it as she strained to the glints.

'Shiny things.'

The chitter of the monochrome magpies heightened as she pulled out tarnished silver and broken pieces of necklaces and handed them to our wide-eyed, wide hands.

'Five for silver, six for gold. Do you know that on the other side of the earth, magpies don't chatter, but flute? And they don't steal, they swoop down and peck out your eyes.'

We flinched. Grandma's stories. Silver, gold, secrets, violence. Keeps you meek and the world magic, keeps you safe, keeps you fed your supper with no complaints, and in bed by eight.

Grandma winked at us and we stepped back as the bickering chutter of magpies scattered in a shimmer of eye-aching blue and ebony.

'Time for tea girls.'

* * * *

Over our bread and jam, grandma taught us the full rhyme. We ran upstairs after supper to the attic to sit cross legged on the floor and face each other. We were captivated by these thoughts of silver and gold and the secret lives of magpies.

'So when you see two magpies, it's good luck?'

'Yes, because they're married.'

'What do you think a magpie wedding is like?'

We are momentarily lost, thinking about this.

'Well, I think they have to bring silver and gold.'

'What sort? In sort of thread and material? Or piles of coins? Or goblets?'

We ponder again.

'Coins have got to be hard for magpies to carry around. Maybe silks they can tie to their ankles like streaming ribbons. And thin pendants they can carry in their beaks. But what about the bad luck?'

'Well, if one is alone, it means his wife has died.'

'Or her husband.'

'But why is it bad luck for three for a girl?'

This is troubling. Are we bad luck too; double bad luck? Were we not supposed to be born? We stare at each other seeking comfort in the endlessly renewing fascination of our matching faces. We are more accustomed to each other's face than our own.

'Maybe it's more simple. It's just a married pair, plus one.'

We look at the floor, doubtful, and pick at our skirt hems in thought. Then a chitter by the window disturbs us and we skip up to lean out of the sash from grandma's attic and watch the magpies going to bed.

* * * *

Grandma combs our hair into bunches which we hate, and we go out into the lane. We skip along holding hands, reciting 'one for sorrow, two for joy.' We stop every time we see magpies to count them and whenever we see a solitary one in its white waistcoat and shiny black jacket, we remember to shout, 'good morning Mr Magpie, how's your wife?' We alternate this with 'Mrs' and 'husband,' to make sure we're fair.

A man stops to watch us throwing bread to the magpies.

'They could be your witch familiars!' he laughs, while grandma frowns. 'Those two look the same. Just like you two.'

We don't really know what a familiar is, but we like the sound of it.

Next door had a cat. It used to chase the magpies and we laughed to see ten of them see it off; 'what's ten magpies grandma?' 'ten for a surprise!' and the cat slunk off to sulk. Grandma told us other versions and used to chase us when we saw 'eight for a kiss!' but it always ended up with the devil somehow.

'Are magpies evil?' we ask each other. We're not sure.

'But it's always two for joy.' We are calmed. Whether three is for a girl or a funeral, the two of us are always for good luck.

* * * *

We go into the forest at night. We planned it for weeks like a midnight feast, like a treasure hunt. We would find the home of the magpies and bring back everything they stole. We imagined reuniting tearful princesses with their jewels, and we would be rewarded like heroes. It felt a bit like a betrayal of the magpies, but maybe we never thought we'd really steal their treasure. We just wanted to see it, shining and heaped up with the magpies dancing round it.

We went into the forest at night.

We went into the forest.

We were afraid in the dark, but we held hands and took turns being the bravest. We reminded ourselves that there are no bears and wolves; those mindless savages that can't be reasoned with or be moved by two little girls in the woods. We were not lost, we marked two notches (two for joy) in a tree every time we changed direction.

Into the forest.

The moon is half full exactly and we can see the ghostly outline of its shadowed half. Black and white, a bit like a magpie. It's a cool night, but not as cold as winter and we have our jumpers on. The forest is thick and shudders around us, leaves whisper and we tighten hands. We follow a crook in the path into a clearing.

And here is the Magpie King and all his court, resplendent in black and white, the green blue shimmers of their feathered coats gleam in the light from a vast pile of silver and gold heaped before him, and all the other magpies skip and flap around. The sound is deafening and the movement of black and white, white and black dizzying until all colour and shapes break down and become each other, identical twins, and we stop pretending to be brave now. The Magpie Court has us in its beak.

When the Magpie King steps forward, we see his silver chain of office resting on his white breast and there are gold ribbons streaming from his legs. Behind is his throne in giddy opal and amethyst and there are pillars framing it in emerald and gold, like the moon floating in the forest. When he speaks, it is the corvid call and chatter.

'What two little girls dare to leave their beds in the middle of the night to wander my forest?'

We look at each other. No heroic plans of returning treasure now. We speak up.

'We wanted to admire your beautiful court. We wanted to see your silver and gold.'

We wanted to tell the lonely magpies not to be sad and give them company.

'So you wanted to gawp at my riches, not bring any?' the king squawks. The talons on his feet gleam and his beak is razor sharp. His eyes widen and the rage swells his huge wings.

We shuffle awkwardly. We apologise. We beg to be allowed to go forth from that place and return again with gifts for the magpies.

'No,' the King's voice ratchets. 'Thieves fear thievery most of all.' He circles us, inspecting us both, our bunches, our socks, our jumpers, his wings barring us from the rest of the forest. 'You have seen our secret to never be told. Now I need a bargain to be sure you won't steal our secrets or our treasure.' And he lunges for us and drags at us and all the magpies peck and push and the world is black and white and sharp and we are pulled apart for the first time in our life.

It always ends with the devil somehow.

'Bring back treasure,' the king commands. 'Before you can leave here together.'

I run alone through the forest.

* * * *

Our eyes are both stinging, we know, and our throats both breathless and shut; we both feel the empty air at our side, but I am so cold in the forest.

Back home I slam through the door sobbing and empty drawers – I have become magpie eyed for shiny things. I scoop up teaspoons, clocks, small figurines, I steal granddad's watch and grandma's wedding rings and pearl earrings from the painted china pots she keeps on her dressing table.

Out again into the night I run with these offerings for the magpie king to pay for my sister back again.

* * * *

Crafty magpie, grandma said. Sly old bird.

Back into the clearing, there are no birds; no opal amethyst throne, no court, no sister. I lay down with my bag of offerings and wait. I watch the moon sink and the sky fade from black to white. I wait until I get hungry, and I get cold and I stay waiting. I wait alone for days with the seven-magpie secret.

Crafty old magpies. They steal things.

In the grey dawn, a single magpie drops onto the branch of the dead oak above me. It chatters mournfully.

One for sorrow.

Life Lessons from Carmella

Carmella was an uncomfortably brash woman. I cringed the first time she came to me, all gap teeth and cleavage with huge, tacky, hooped earrings, and smoking incessantly. She didn't talk so much as bray, and her voice was nasal. '*Guarda, cara!* We have to get you something to eat; look at those skinny tits!'

I found her coarse.

To be honest, I didn't much like her. I had hoped for a more refined and graceful sort of benefactress, plump and reassuring, yet with a sort of stately wisdom. Because wisdom and dignity should emanate from a godmother, along with her magic, she is a queen of a sort, after all; in her own way. That was what I expected. Someone suited to me. Someone to recognise my own sensitivities and delicacies, someone to help my inner grace and charm to blossom, to nourish my beauty and elegance. Along with glorious gowns and coaches, I had thought she would help to polish my manners, give me stern but affectionate advice on what to say to show myself as coquettish but clever, modest yet educated. That is what I wanted.

What I got was a damn good shock the first time I heard a whistle from the window and a coy voice cooing '*ciaooo bellaaa.*' And there was this woman, leering sordidly in through the open glass, her great, fat cleavage heaped up on the frame. Honestly. She crashed in through the door so heavily it made me shudder, and settled herself, knees wide open, on a stool by the fire. One hand was firmly on her thigh while the other gesticulated with her cigarette. I coughed, politely at first, but soon enough it was hard to keep my spluttering ladylike as she continued puffing away, her other arm flailing expressions, flicking ash on the floor that I kept diving to sweep up. Ironic addition on my nickname.

From her stool (it was my stool, mine, the only place I had for repose), she asked a hundred questions; short ones that only require a word or two in response, and she gave her opinion on everything. This place is a dump, she said, a real … well, her language was filthy; and she'd seen the way I'd been treated, and she could read my heart, she said. I couldn't imagine such a person could read the finer feelings in the aching heart of a cultivated girl, but she told me she could, and what she thought of my family. She used many vicious gestures when she did that, and there I went with my dustpan again. By the time she finally left, I had a nervous headache and had to lie down.

I don't know what she expected of me. I don't know why she elected on me for her favours, such as they were. On her later visits through her stream of alarming jokes and innuendo, she fiercely insisted that she could see my potential, what I could become, and that I had it in me, deep down, to be really good. I was never sure what she meant by that, I already have the most sweet and mild disposition of the family, and in those early days I found myself wondering if she wasn't some kind of disreputable madam attempting to recruit me for the most shameful of things. If only her language hadn't been so despicable.

She was a talker. I hoped for someone who would listen and be gentle; even hug me. It's been a long time since my mamma died. She *did* try to hug me several times, but I always winced when she advanced, all cheap perfume and foul smoke, with her over-rouged lips that I thought would stain my linen or clog my pores with cheap grease.

Then after that fight with my stepmother, I was picking chickpeas out of the beans, both of which had been thrown over the floor. I don't know how long Carmella watched me before I noticed she was there. *Ey*, she said, and the throaty utterance startled me so that I dropped all the peas and had to start again. I leaned back on my heels to give my thighs – tensed from kneeling – a rest, and tried to compose my face into something patient and pleasant. Always make your face nice, mamma used to tell me. I looked up at her, leaning over the half open stable door to the kitchen. Carmella took a drag on her cigarette then flicked the ash behind her and spat. *Quella stronsa*, she sneered. I blushed at the vivid insult to my stepmother, and picked at the peas again. *Minchia, che stronsa*, she said again shaking her head. I picked chickpeas. I heard the door bang open with the full violence of her anger and her heels rung on the flagstones until her booted feet filled my view. Why do you put up with it, she asked me. *Devi dirla va fan culo.* I crimsoned, muttered that obedience is a virtue, and a lady never says such things. *Merda*, she said, you're not a lady, you're a slave. I blinked back the tears. She flicked her cigarette and ground ash, pea and pulse underfoot. I'll tell her myself, she said, and slammed the door as she left. I stared at smashed mess on the floor and threw myself into the hearth's ashes and wept.

When grief had finally exhausted itself, I wearily staggered back to the pulses. To my surprise, the beans and chickpeas were on the long table, neatly separated into two terracotta bowls.

Carmella visited often. Sometimes she helped. While I was hanging out linen, blinding white in the windy sunshine, she handed me pegs from a mysterious pocket that never seemed to have anything in it; apparently so she could follow me more easily to talk at. But mainly she sat on the stool or a tree stump to talk. She said such alien things, so thoroughly against anything I'd ever known. She pointed out turtle doves in the pear trees and told me they form strong pair bonds for one breeding season and have up to six broods in a year. Then she said something very crude, and I gasped. She started explaining from whence a baby came, how it is

7

formed, how it got there and how you can encourage or prevent it. Horrified yet drawn, I tried to drown her voice by shouting that I was but a maid, I should not know of these things until my wedding day. *Minchia, cara*, she said, you want to wait till then? I was confused and started to cry, at which she tapped me smartly on the thigh and told me to pull myself together.

One afternoon she came upon me under the hazel tree. My stepsisters had been particularly cruel that day and I had gone to pray under its green skirts that I had planted on my mother's grave from a sprig that my father snapped on his way back from market. I prayed and often wept here, watering that vivid bush with tears, and was rewarded at least with the sweetness of its nuts. I heard Carmella whistling a tune, and then her shadow was over me. I squinted up into the sunlight to see her, shading my eyes. *Cosa successa?* She asked. I began to cry again, and she sighed and hefted her corpulent body down onto the daisies. She leaned her back against the lower branches with a faint groan and scuffed at the dirt until she turned up the fat, rich nuts. She cracked them; tossing them into her mouth and chewing noisily. *Allora?* She said, at last. Tears fell again. This time she was gentle. Serious; not trying to make light of anything or pull me up. Just waited.

I told her. About my sisters following me like schoolgirls, whispering loudly until I could bear it no more. Then shouting triumphantly that they had met my father long before they met *me*. *Long* before. I asked them what they meant, and they looked sly. Then they pelted me with small stones from their pockets shouting, 'the good girl never tells, the good girl never says anything!' and as they struck me, I saw my father pass through a door at the end of the corridor. I told Carmella how he looked at me, weeping from a cut on my brow, my sisters laughing horribly; then looked away. I watched him turn his back and walk off to the library. Then I came here.

She gathered me to her bosom then and rocked me, crooning in her flat accents. This time, for the first time, I clung on. *Cattivo*, she said, over and over. Wicked, wicked.

I calmed eventually. I must be patient, I must be good, I said, drying my eyes. If I am always good and gentle, pure and obedient, God will protect me. That's what mamma said. *Jesus*, sighed Carmella. *Che palle.* Your mother is buried underneath us and instead of God, you have me. She told me that sometimes wicked men run off with other women and trade old families for new, but I must never put up with that sort of thing. Love is not love without respect. I sighed, said I wasn't sure what that had to do with papa. She rolled her eyes and tried again. Said that if I could be happy with myself as a person, then a man would not want to run off after someone else. And if he did, it wouldn't matter to me. Besides that, she said, if he ever did, she'd *tagliare via il suo cazzo*. Affronted, I told her I *was* happy with myself. I was a good person, pure and sweet. She said she got the feeling I didn't think I deserved much better. And I still had to work some things out about myself. I shrugged helplessly. She tossed me a shelled hazel and we ate the moist nuts together. She asked me if I knew how to make pleasure for myself, and huddled over to me on her knees with another hazelnut, using her little finger to point to certain areas and began rubbing it. I shrieked and ran off, grabbed a pail from the water butt and threw it at her. She raced after me with surprising speed for a large woman and eventually dunked me, posterior first into the trough, shouting *stronsa!* in my face, helpless with laughing. Good and pure, she mocked, *ma donna*. Your mother will spin in her grave.

I always carried a hazelnut in my pocket after that. I don't know why.

What do you want, *tu?* She interrogated one day. She was at the bench in the kitchen, up to her elbows in flour. I spun eggs round idly on the table and shrugged. I don't know what I want, I told her; to be free of this one day, I suppose. To be rescued, to marry, I smiled. To be a Contessa – rich and wealthy! Carmella's thick arms and knuckles pummelled and punched the bread dough and I flinched as the table rattled. *Perche?* She asked me. She slammed the dough down again and I ducked. She tutted. *Tranquilla, regazza.* Well, I begged, be gentle if you want me to keep still! You're too weak girl. You need metal in your back. And more thoughts in your head wouldn't do you any harm. I need patience, not iron, I retorted. You need to shift for yourself, she said, ripping fistfuls of dough off the pile and throwing them down again in choking clouds of dust. My anger flared, patience is virtuous! I shouted. I'm being obedient and pure. Even in the face of your filthy influence! She took offence at this. Threw the dough in the bowl so it spun a full minute, crazily. Told me that controlling your own destiny didn't make you evil; told me she was the only person who really cared about my happiness, and she was trying to help me get it without waiting around for someone else. She flounced out of the kitchen, swearing at me again over her shoulder and aggressively scrubbing her hands on her apron. And piercing through relief, I was surprised to feel a sense of sadness cut me as I watched the wideness of her retreating back. Then I was alone; only a pillar of curling smoke was left where she had stood.

A month later arrived the time of the La Festa Primavera. I remember as a young child my mamma tying blue ribbons in my hair and taking me in a white dress to watch the dancing. Girls from local villages were decked in flowers to celebrate the spring and would process through the town, then assemble to dance on the green. There would be little cakes and lemonade and many games.

I had not gone for years.

I watched them setting up, hoisting the huge, be-ribboned pole in the centre of the square. My basket was filled with the day's shopping and I rested it in front of my clogged feet while I took a few moments in the sunshine to watch. I could feel Carmella sidling up to me, heralded by her familiar scent of cheap fragrance and cigarettes. She had not visited since we fought and I was nervous to smile my full and unexpected joy at seeing her again, lest she rebuke me or, worse, leave. I enjoyed the meditative quiet as she smoked while we stood side by side, watching the men guiding the pole. She flicked the ash and said, you know what that pole symbolises, right? The lechery was her olive branch, and I snorted my laughter aloud. I can guess, I smirked. She winked and dug me in the ribs; started hopping about in a sort of dance celebrating the 'beautiful fertility of the season,' as she put it.

Suddenly she stopped. Continued to smoke and watch. There'll be a big ball, you know. I do know, I replied. The court always holds three balls over the holiday, one each night. All the gentry are invited. I stiffened and took a deep breath. My family are going. She puffed again. *E tu?* Not me, I replied crisply. *Lo vedremo*, she replied. We'll see.

Although I had seen that screaming tantrums generally got my sisters what they wanted, I knew that wouldn't work for me. So I kept control of my dignity when, inspired by the conspiratorial eyebrow waggles of Carmella and her gentle pressings, I renewed my pleas to my stepmother to accompany her to the ball. The three of them were in her dressing room when I entered with a decanter of wine, and their excitement was infectious, pure, and childlike. Hard to imagine cruelty in such genuine joy.

I complimented them on their beauty. I praised their rich chocolate coloured hair, the way their jewels perfectly enhanced the grace of their jaws and collar bones. How their silks complemented their complexions and how artifice so perfectly accentuated natural charm. They preened, smugly. I poured them wine, smiling, laughing at their joy. Could I come too, and watch you dance?

How quickly those faces changed; three sets of shoulders locking together like a wall in a colour chart of pistachio, dusk and peach. They laughed, again so helplessly, I almost laughed too. What would you wear, they asked? Your clogs? I inclined my head; lowered my eyes submissively. Perhaps one of my beautiful sisters would lend me an old season's gown. We're similar statures. Then I could enjoy your happiness.

My stepmother's face was cold with disdain while her daughters were warm with scorn. She stepped close to me and spoke softly in my ear. You are part of this family only on sufferance, she breathed. A hanger-on. A blight from the past we wanted to leave behind. Her voice gathered emotion now, and cracked as she continued. When your father and I married, we wanted a fresh start, and every day we see you, you take a little of that happiness away. I am close to persuading him to remove you to a convent. You will *never* be a part of us.

Here my father entered the room, handsome in his finest weeds, with genuine radiance on his face. Looking from my sisters to him, their resemblance was clear. He stopped short, on seeing me, like the light had gone out of him, his joy crumpled like paper. Papa, I breathed, softly. I'd so love to come and share in all your joy. I looked him right in the face. Let me join you, Father.

He cleared his throat awkwardly, looked at his wife and flushed. Muttered something about it not being appropriate. I took a deep breath. I could almost smell cigarettes in the air. I am still your child, father. He could not look at me. Legally, I pressed. Here, all four of them flared up and hustled me out of the room amid incoherent shrieks and shoves.

The sunset that evening was splendid, and I sat sniffling under the hazelnut tree looking at it. After I'd finished wallowing in self-pity, I had a bit of a talk with myself. The way Carmella might. I thought how my adjective choice to my father was calculated only to hurt which was neither loving, nor good, seeing as I seemed to set such store by goodness. Perhaps if being good *was* so important, then perhaps it is important to be good to those we love who are not good, and if we can still love them anyway, so much the better. Then perhaps I am separate from them, independent, my sense of me not so tied up in them. I thought about my wish to go to the ball which was just silly frippery anyway; a vain and shallow thing. It is to celebrate the spring, and here I was under the hazel blossom by the pear trees, watching the turtle doves, which was much better really. I smiled in the fading light. Perhaps I could be happy if only I could choose when to enjoy these things, and if I could live where I was not seen as a guilty stain, for all my efforts at goodness, which was really maybe just jealousy, or even something I had not thought about properly before.

Carmella approached as Venus rose. For the first time, I smiled widely at her as she hefted herself up the slope towards me.

She was more garish than ever. *Buona serrata, bellezza!* I grinned. Celebrating spring heartily, godmother? She toppled down next to me, and flattened out on the dewing grass, arms spread wide, with a happy sigh. Then she was upright and looking dead at me. I see you've been thinking, she said. Wanted to know if I'd asked to attend the ball, and what had happened. I told her. She grinned. Called me a *gatto* for my first ever sharp tongued pride and self-assertion. Then she grabbed me by my wrists and hopped up, dragging me up after her. She inspected me, pulling at my hair, licking her thumb and smearing it over smudges on my face, poking and squeezing at my breasts, torso, backside and thighs. Stop, I laughed, you know I'm a prude; what're you up to! She stood back a pace then, towards the tree. Seized her jug of wine and took a swig, handed it to me, and I drank too. She stamped three times on my mamma's grave, then she looked up to the turtledoves in the tree and called. They both landed on her outstretched arm, and sat there,

11

kissing. I looked on in wonder as she whispered to them, then jolted her arm and they flew back up to the branches. As they landed, she threw her body against the hazel and rubbed and cackled and shouted and laughed and the birds set up a racket and the branches shivered and bent crazily and blossom, acres of blossom like snow, like stars, tumbled over my head. I looked up and closed my eyes as they fell over my face.

Allora, came the triumphant voice of Carmella. I opened my eyes and smiled at her. The white blossom seemed to be everywhere, carpeting the ground, strung above me, and glowing in the corner of my eyes. Then I looked down – to see I was covered in it, adorned in it, a gorgeous white gown shimmering against my skin. When I looked up again at Carmella in joy and gratitude, her face was transported in such a way I'd never seen. Admiration, emotion, joy, loss, all at once. She nodded, curtly, but I leapt on her; crushed her close and wept on that marvellous, enormous bosom. *Attenzione!!* She shrieked, smoothing out my skirts. Then she delved her hand into an unseen pocket of my dress and pulled out my little hazelnut. She tossed it high in the air and clapped, and there was a splendid coach and four. She opened the door and shoved me in. Remember everything I've told you, she said. And be home by midnight or you'll be out wearing nothing but nuts. And away I sped.

My father is a rich man, but such splendour in the court I have never seen. I was too young to attend the ball when my mamma was alive, and of course, had never attended as a young woman. The grand hall was luxuriously festooned in wreathes of flowers that wrapped gorgeously round its pillars and a thousand candles twinkled warm light on every face. Sweet, almost sickly scents of rose and orange blossom pulsed through the air which was thick with music, chatter, laughter and the clatter of glasses and plates.

Sta notte, sono una donna chi sceglie il suo destino I thought; a woman who chooses, and took a deep breath before striding into the hall. Faces turned, people clustered towards me, women wanted to talk to me, ask about my home, my education, men wanted to dance with me, and dance and talk I did, swirling in giddy joy in the bright room into the warm spring night. Such freedom! I saw my family and swished past them, smiling. They recognised me. Of course they did. Or their faces wouldn't have paled so. I tried not to be satisfied that it had rather spoiled their night; it would be ungracious when I was so happy. Carmella was there, raising a glass, or at times, so I thought, and I kept a weather eye on the clock the size of a dining table, hung above the staircase.

One hour before midnight, dancing stopped, and I caught my breath. Then an announcement I did not hear properly, a gasp from the crowds, which parted, and the prince was suddenly before me. On his face I recognised something of Carmella's expression when she beheld me in the hazel gown, and we danced together for the next hour. As midnight was ripe as the moon for striking, I excused myself and ran out of there, sprung into the coach and made off for home. The coach disintegrated first, and I was running through the fields, tearing my dress on poppies which shivered back into unconnected blossoms, and I finally dashed through the kitchen door, naked as the day I was born, where Carmella was waiting, and collapsed, laughing, into her arms.

The next day my father summoned me. Asked me directly if I had been at the ball; crept out of the house like a guilty thing – stolen a dress from somewhere – and followed them. Out of spite. His tone was cruel and when I gave him the lie, no, father, not I, it wasn't a lie really, for it wasn't the daughter he knew that was there at the ball. Not the meek, obedient, pure, and good daughter, despised for the guilt she provoked; but an older one, who made quips about illegitimacy, who laughed more readily and looked beyond cruelty to a sunset where she was free.

I denied it outright.

The next evening, I was waiting beneath the tree when Carmella arrived; already down to my shift, and she shook the pear trees over my hips and breasts, and I was resplendent in spring's green and gold. Another wink, a slap on the rump and off to the ball I went. The prince sought me out earlier and we danced for hours, save for when we paused to catch our breath and strolled on the balconies for air under the soft, silvery moonlight. I didn't even see my family.

The following morning, all swipes and violences were quietened. No one was forthcoming with orders nor scorn, and, with little to do, I strolled out to the green and watched the children dance around the maypole. The amethyst coloured curtains of a fortune-teller caught my eye, and as I strolled past, I espied Carmella within, hooped earrings now more appropriate with a gold turban and red muslin. She waved. I winked. Later that evening we shook gold and silver over my body, and I danced dizzying sequins. The prince was nice. A handsome man had never been kind to me before. The attention was wonderful. I thought I might be in love.

In my mad dash to race nudity that final night, the silver slipper slipped off somewhere on the balustrade staircase, but I pelted back to Carmella. I told her about the shoe; asked her what might happen. This is your moment now, she said. *Decidi tu.*

Hawthorn was resolute in the hedgerows when I heard the prince was looking for 'the woman of the silver slipper.' I waited under the hazel tree by my mother's grave to talk to Carmella. She did not come.

I had been summoned to my stepmother's chamber to bring ice and bandages. On opening the door and seeing the sight within, I shrieked and dropped the jug which smashed over the floor. I lunged for my sister and knocked the knife from her hand, but I was late, too late – blood drenched the soft Persian rugs, and all my tears could not wash it away.

What have you done?

The prince is here. My stepmother's voice was urgent. He'll marry the girl whose foot fits this slipper, and the girl's is too large by a toe. She will not need to walk on foot if she's a queen.

I could see the woman's chest heaving, trying to force down her own vomit, trying to be resolute for her child whose future she so desperately needed to secure. I suppose I knew all about that. I looked from her to my stepsister, *my* sister I understood at last; our father's younger child.

I spat at her mother: You would harm the child you love by cutting pieces off her like a pig's offal? Diminish her, make her smaller, cut her up until she fits something *you think she must fit*? I suppose she must be silent and obedient through it all too, like a good girl?

I knelt by my weeping sister and held her heaving shoulders against my breast, kissing her curls to comfort. God save us from fathers; and from mothers, too. Then I strode out of the room and down to the hall where the prince waited. I demanded the slipper. My family filed in behind, aghast. Snatching it from his hand; all glamour of evening candles and roses evaporated in the bright morning, I balanced on one foot and slipped it on. There, I said. His face lit up. He sunk to his knees and took my hand. I stepped back a pace; Soft, I snapped. Sire, with a little effort, vicious or otherwise, it will fit each of my pretty sisters, too. Do you really mind which of us you have, so long as it fits? Will you base a lifetime on the chance of a shoe?

I looked at my father. My stepmother – the one he had always loved, all along. I turned back to the prince. I wouldn't risk it, I told him, and I snatched off the slipper and smashed it on the ashen hearth. I marched to my father and faced him, square.

Give me my dowry, I demanded. You owe me that.

I never became a Contessa, or a Principessa. I bought a small mill with my dowry, which was successful, and I gathered a comfortable fortune. I spent liquid summer evenings on the doorstep with friends who would gossip and chatter in the drunk scent of pear blossom and hazel nut. I had children in time, and gathered many other children to me, each loved as wonderful to themselves. I never saw Carmella again. But when the star of Venus rose on spring evenings, I would raise my wine to the heavens and salute her. The old rascal. Then I swore I could even smell cigarettes in the air.

Bread and Roses

There once was a woman who lived with her child on the edge of a pine forest by an open meadow. For three months every year, forest and field were blessed with hyssop flowers and oxlip while the sun never surrendered its hold on the earth but only dipped below the horizon for brief respite. The rest of the year was cold, and snow billowed around the trunks in soft, thick shapes and it was the meadow flowers that slumbered.

The woman walked everywhere, and knitted. From childhood, she cultivated her skill and knitted thick socks, long blankets, bright shawls, fine skirts and jackets. She was popular in the village between the meadows for her gifts, and her beautiful creations of rich teal or deep maroon smeared colour on the blank white of the winter; broke the ache in the eye. One night, when the woman was yet a girl, she wove her first pictogram into the garment. A round bread loaf circled by roses. It was a lovely image and it struck her in that moment that whatever is necessary, like bread and jackets, must also be beautiful. She stored this in her heart from that night.

About this time, she had a friend who spun with the distaff, and another who wove at the loom. But she found that knitting with the thick wool from her bag allowed her to roam freely through the pine forests and plains; her craft was tied to her, rather than she tied to it like her friends to theirs. And thus, she walked. Away from her friends, who had become woven to their homes and new husbands, away from the village and her home, and walked wild, though knit-warm, through the forest. Then on these adventures, she got with child, and such are the minds of such villages that no more could she return, warmly, to the friends and family who had never so walked.

In the brief summer of her boy's second year, she took him to the brook in the pines. The spring melt had passed, and the brook burbled to the child who paddled on fat feet in its cool shallows. The woman sang to him, and knitted a hood for the winter, in emerald and sun-bright gold to keep up his heart through the cold months. She watched him giggle and stamp, with the little sleeves of his blue jumper pulled up as he bent to splash his hands in the water.

A shriek from her child stopped her song. Looking up, she saw a leveret struggling mightily in the curve of the stream. At once her eyes took in the racing hare along the bank in blind panic for its young, and the chubby legs of her child as he waded into the deeper water to catch the half-drowned creature. The boy wavered unsteady in the swift torrent's swirl – she threw down her knitting and lunged to the water. Just as he lost his footing, she scooped him up, along with the leveret which had butted against his calves, and in her desperate snatch, had come to rest in his lap.

On the bank, her skirts all drenched and chilled, she calmed herself between scolding the boy for carelessness, and kissing him for relief and his kind heart. Then she swept off his blue jumper and wrapped the leveret inside. Together, they watched it dry and twitch, and eventually revive. The woman pulled off her own jumper to keep her son warm in the great pines' shade, and the leveret bounced from her lap, and ran thither to the waiting hare.

Happy in that reprieve after averted disaster, and with the sun on her bare shoulders, the woman took up her song and knitting again. But now something strange happened. The hare approached and began to writhe, and before her astonished eyes, it swelled and grew until it was the shape of a woman, but with leaves for hair, skin like bark and eyes the hazel of nuts. The woman gaped; her needles abandoned on her lap.

'You saved my child,' the wood sprite said. 'And for love of mine, you sacrificed your own child's fur. Thank you.'

The woman fumbled, and awkwardly tried to shield her bareness. She murmured, 'He is yet warm; it was no trouble.'

'Still,' spoke the sprite, her voice the susurration of wind in pine needles, 'I am thankful, and I will reward you.' The woman stared, aghast at this. 'Your craft saved my child. Now you will be able to knit anything from anything.'

'What?' the woman sprang after her, but the sprite had vanished with only a rustle and a shadow that may have been a hare pounding away between moss-covered stones.

Her amazement was broken by her child, who piled a handful of peridot moss and heather in her damp lap. Smiling, he tottered off, picking more little trophies to give his mother; a cone, a dry leaf, a forget-me-not growing in a patch of sun. The woman held up the moss in her hand and stared at it, her knitting needles in the other. She poked the soft, earthy green. And to her amazement, it sprung to her needles and cast on. She stared at the looped tufts, then tried a stitch. As she flashed her needles in the sunlight, a beautiful green bodice was knitted. She stitched in the purple heather in a border around the low neck, then put it on. Together, the woman and her son walked back towards the village.

Now she took to knitting on the green to amuse the village children, knitting them fancies from whatever they brought her. One gathered flowers from around the meadows and she cast them onto her needles and knitted a fragrant sash. Another brought twigs, and she knitted a mat. Another walked carefully from the well holding a weak pool of water in his cupped hands. The woman looked up and smiled, then cast on the droplets and knitted him a silver handkerchief.

Now her transgression was overlooked and she was again loved by her village, whose people gathered round her arbour with wilder things for her to knit. Dresses from green leaves, bridges from branches, horseshoes from iron, skirts from flames, tapestries from rainbows and fishing nets from raindrops; even moonlight she cast on to her needles and knitted plates and cups and silver cloaks. And as she wove the fantastic into the useful, all bore the little motif of the loaf and roses. Her old friends came while she knitted and sang, one with the distaff, the other with embroidery, and they gossiped and laughed while their children played with her son.

In the way of things, this could not last. Winter came; the sun dribbled the last of its gold beneath the horizon, and the snows returned. Ice stood in splayed crowns on bare hedges and dead river reeds and the light came only from the brightness of snow and the writhing opal of the Aurora. The king, of course, had heard of the woman's talents, and one blue, starlit morning he sent a soldier to fetch her. In her childhood her mother had sung her stories of girls who lost their voices while cursed to weave shirts for their enchanted bird brothers, and she was afraid. Woman's work. But her work was portable, curses must play out, and she had her song. She steeled herself, left her boy to learn weaving with her friend, and went with the soldier.

She was brought before the king. He showed her a vast chamber full of straw and bade her knit it to gold, or she would be executed at the hour of dawn. She sat the whole night knitting – there was so much straw – she sang all the songs she knew to calm her spirit and she wove the summer memory of sunlight into her knitting. By morning, piled and folded, were bolts and bolts of gold cloth.

The king was pleased. The next night he showed her a chamber of white linen. He bade her knit it to rich silver, or on the morrow, she would die. She sighed then and looked at the king's blue lips and dark frown. Cold, in his granite palace, cold in all his useless wealth and arctic in his heart. Greed is a terrible thing. Yet she sat the night and knitted silver coins, great goblets, tinkling torques and sparkling necklaces from the silver-tainted, moonlit linen. And her heart was heavy; no motif did she stitch in the corner because all her work, though beautiful, was useless.

The next morning the king surveyed her work with a grim smile.

'One more task for you, woman,' he said. 'Knit me the black opal of the Aurora into a cloak. I want its power on my shoulders, that all will tremble at me and know I am king of the north.'

The woman cast down her eyes and sighed.

'If you can do this,' he continued, 'you will be free to return to your village.'

The woman raised her chin and looked him full in the face; her needles crossed in front of her.

'Really?' she said. 'You have seen what I can do, and with all your greed, you will but just let me go?'

The king took his eyes off his silver and looked her up and down.

'Watch your tongue, whore.' He took in her moonlight knitted robe, its motif blazoned on the hip, the cloak; thick and rich of knitted cloud. Resolving, he narrowed his eyes. 'Take the wench back to her cell. She'll need accustom herself to it.'

That night, the woman knitted the cloak on a long rainbow-coloured, twisting thread from the sky. When it was done, she gazed a while on the glimmering, shifting garment that was so beautiful, it made her catch her breath. Then she put it aside.

She took her wool from her bag, soft with hints of summer; buttercups, cowslips and moss green. She knitted a tunic that a steward might wear, comfortable to move through the forest to husband the oaks, gather mushrooms, fish for a family, to warm a child; beautifully woven with pinecone stitching at the borders, and the motif of bread and roses at the breast. A garment to save him, to untie the corruption in his heart, to remind him that a King must be useful, as well as glorious.

The next morning, she presented the king with the cloak. His eyes glittered in the shimmering colours and he stretched out his hands.

'Tarry, sir.'

The king dragged his eyes away from the cloak to her face, and the garment of summer greens in her other hand.

'I offer you this tunic freely. You are cold, alone here in your castle. This garment is thick and warm; it will be comfortable when you ride your horse to bring aid to your people, when you lead them in battle, in winter, in hunger; this will suit you better. If you wear it and ride, it will bring you the warmth and the love you seek more than the other. Take it.'

But the king's eyes slipped from the gentle tunic and pulled towards the flaming robe. He stretched his arms out again.

'Give it me.'

The king seized the robe. He wrapped it around himself and gaped at the beautiful reflection in the glass, his madness twisting his face to a leer. The woman stepped back and took out her needles. From the black shadows of that cold hall, she knitted a dark cloak to hide herself, and slipped away unnoticed. Behind her, the aurora mantle, made of untamed fire that twists and thrashes on winter nights, spun and writhed and shone till it would not sit upon his shoulders but enveloped his head and whipped around his mouth and eyes and ears till his whole body was one beautiful, shimmering flame. He struggled to smooth it down and pull his head free, but it was too strong. Bright light and his strangled cries filled the grey hall, until both went out together.

The woman walked back to the warm homes of her friends in the village, singing and knitting.

Crow Mother

For aunties and surrogates everywhere
And for Reuben

Everyone, and no one, understands the mystery of birth. It is a superlative creation that any woman can do, if she wants to. Pouring living things out of her, slimy things that wriggle and scream – unlike the dry dead promises of men.

It is something animal and entirely Godly. The screams and grunts a woman makes as her eyes darken to a deep and primal place to bring forth her child, are more abandoned than any an animal can muster. Like dancing; primal and poetic – birthing is too. The wild circles of cries painted in the air – blended whorls of relief, pain, wonder.

This is not a Christmas story. But a child was born.

*****

He came into the world and blinked – huge black myopic eyes. They tell me all babies are glass blue-eyed when they're born.

He was not.

His cave-black eyes reflect the dark, safe womb and he stares down at the shadowed table – for comfort. The world is so cold, so loud, so hard. Everything hurts. His skin is as soft as insides and instead we show him edges. Horrified, he screams his way into the world and only those soft dark things – flesh, crevices, darkness comfort him against a world so sharp, so bright, and green it hurts.

Mother crow heard him cry. All crows and ravens are mothers and aunts and when they hear a baby cry their breasts tug, their lower parts hurt, and it wells together to engender their desperate wailing caw.

No crow can hear a child cry without pouring out her own wail in compassion and pity.

*****

The little child was loved, so loved, and he was dressed in white and laid in his cradle in the garden in the shade of a great eucalyptus tree. The breeze stirred the leaves to peek through and whispered 'oh! What a lovely child!' And the tree jealously wrapped round its trailing tresses so it could keep the child to itself. The bees loved the flowers then followed the budding glow of the child and said to each other 'he izzz lovely' and the flowers craned their necks to look at him. Birds flitted down to sing him lullabies.

22

The child dimly smelled milk and honey. Colours were bright and smudgy. In the glow, he felt better – much better. The sun was warm and soft on his little cheeks; his blankets were soft and edgeless and this new sensation of the gentle breeze and birdsong was lovely to his sightless eyes.

The bees and the trees and the craning clematis and all the flowers agreed he was beautiful, beautiful and they loved him deeply.

And in the garden, under the apple tree, the fairies felt it. They heard the talk of the flowers and the bees and trees and the birds and resolved to take this beautiful baby for their own.

*****

A woman – animal – primal – civilized – creator – walks into her garden with a book and milk; milk for her child.

The cradle is empty.

Her wail lifts and pierces the grey sky.

*****

In fairy land, the changeling child is doted on and loved. Fairies bring him nectar and tickle his toes. They sing to him. He is rocked in a cradle woven with dog roses and willowherb and the hawthorn fragrance soothes him on the bank by the stream. The bee sucks at the cowslip and the baby sleeps.

Are fairies wicked? Are they parts of nature? Is the bee wicked for taking the pollen from the rose? We devise romances – she is the go-between, waggling her dance with the joy of spring, passing love notes between rose and apple blossom until, soaked in warm sun and scent, they meld together. Maybe this is like what fairies do.

Or maybe if you are left alone too long, they steal babies away to fairy land out of jealousy – like Oberon jealous of Titania's changeling boy – and refuse to give them back.

*****

The little child had serious eyes. He awoke to find he was surrounded by ladybirds, moths, and newts. He cast his dark eyes down because he remembered his milk and scented mother and she was not there. Then with a crinkling of his smooth brow, like silk crumpled, he closed his eyes on flower and fairy, opened his mouth, and cried.

Mother crow, black, huge mother, felt his cry pierce her heart and opened her beak to wail.

Mother crow sobbed and wept at the despair of the little child. She hopped down, heavy from her high branch and crept, silver-eyed towards him. She laid down her head on his tiny chest and nestled there, burrowed there, her eyes closed while her crystal tears moistened his cheeks and fists. She put her head on his aching heart and felt it – took it – as she nudged in.

And in her love and pity, her own heart broke.

Hearing the fading suspiration of her last cry, the other crows flocked down from their high perches, desperate for their sister who had died for the sadness of a human baby. They set up their wail in chorus till the echo lanced through every fairy and every human above, and all were misted with a terrible sadness that stopped both in a moment that ripped through all spaces. And with feather dark and heavy hearts, the crows gently lifted the baby, their sister still on his breast, and carried the boy home to his mother.

Mother crow – who loves children so much she keens in despairing fellow feeling when she hears a baby cry – was carried home with the changeling child and brought out of fairy land, back to the garden. Mother crow laid open-eyed and dead upon his breast, her silver and crystal tears on his heart, but he slept; comforted, with his tiny arm around her wing.

Mother came out into the garden and rejoiced in the sunlight to find her beautiful child restored.

Sensitivity

'There's blood here,' Tessa muttered into the steaming sink.

'What?' Myrtle looked over, shoving damp hair away from her eyes with the crook of her elbow. 'Another miscarriage?' The grey-haired woman looked up from the mangle.

'Bring it over.'

Tessa pulled the sopping sheet out of the tub and wrenched it in twists to ring out the excess water. Holding it out and leaning back against its weight, she heaved it over.

The older woman absently cleared thinned hair from her face. She gripped the folds of the sheet in both hands, holding a portion of the stain flat. Her green eyes narrowed with concentration.

'No, the stain is too dark and it's very high on the sheet.' She pulled another handful of the linen up into view. 'And this is menses, further down.' Her eyes locked Tessa's as she handed the sheet back. The silence smothered the washroom as Myrtle also paused her scrubbing, and all three women looked at each other over the blood-smeared sheet with set jaws, flinching.

'Just clean it,' the older woman directed.

Tessa gathered it up in slow armfuls and hefted it back into the sink. She reached for the brush and stone and held them still in her hands for a moment, eyes closed. Then she spat over her shoulder.

'It's nearly every week now.'

Myrtle looked up too, and slapped her brush against the tub's side. 'And it's just—'

'Clean it.'

Tessa scrubbed in harsh, sharp brushes and the stain began to diminish. As if all the misery and ugliness in the world could be cleaned away just like a stain on a sheet. And only a little effort and pain, as her knuckles hit the side of the tub and the flesh of her palm was pinched in the violence of her scrubbing. Myrtle chewed her lips and sniffed as she wrung sheets until her hands hurt. Over it all hung the faint creaking of the mangle as the older woman turned the handle. Rotating it rhythmically to impose order on a wrinkled sheet and a rumpled world; to smooth out and remove her sorrows and those of that girl upstairs, shivering alone on her tower bed.

All three minds wandered through different passageways to the princess, newly wed. Tessa thought of the ceremony, Myrtle of the girl's arrival, drenched from a violent storm; the older woman pondered the first miscarriage. And all thought of the desire in the Prince's cruel eyes and the delicacy of the pale girl.

Myrtle cleared her throat. 'It's been over a year since she came now.'

'No,' Tessa corrected, 'It was just bad weather that week. She arrived late summer, and it's only spring now.'

'Oh yes,' Myrtle nodded. 'August rain can be as bad as November; the clouds drop, and you wouldn't know the difference.' Her eyes glazed again. 'She was so straight-backed back then, wasn't she? You could tell she was beautiful even though her hair was plastered to her face and her cloak soaked with mud nearly to the elbow. And she never cringed in her wet things as she moved; she was…' Myrtle stared at the high ceiling again, searching for the word. 'Proud. In the way she walked I mean.' Tessa grunted her assent, now taking longer, slower strokes at the sheet. 'And she spoke nice. Quietly, but assured. Kind. They should have worked it out from that.'

'But there has to be the Test,' the old woman spat.

Of course. There must be the Test. Tension had been bubbling and steaming on the borders for months and always the anxiety for an heir, an heir. Three years the Kingdom spent searching for a powerful alliance while skirmishes broke out blocking trade lines until they were all but cut off; and the Queen despairing while her son rode out to the borders to slake his lust on peasant girls the other side. And then arrived this bedraggled woman, claiming to be a Princess from a wealthy Kingdom, begging for a night's board with pledges of great royal recompense. She was already susceptible; fleeing from attackers on the road with her servants killed – alone, in need. She could be compelled to marry. Then alliance, an heir, stability. But to be sure. So with a painted smile, the Queen led the girl after dinner to her bedchamber, heaped with mattresses. Twenty stacked to the ceiling; the Princess lying there like a fresco painter for the worst night's sleep of her life.

'Just a little pea under all those mattresses,' the old woman murmured over the turning mangle.

'Just a little prick,' Tessa sneered.

'Tess…' faltered Myrtle, wincing.

'Fie, she looked worse the next morning than when she came in out the storm! Her eyes were hunted and black. And how she struggled down those stairs! She came here in need. How could they be so cruel to someone so helpless?'

'Oh, these aristocrats are a cold lot I'd say,' Myrtle suggested. 'And is it not a Princess's duty to be sensitive; to… endure, silently, for her Kingdom? And then she owed them, so she had to pledge to them. But when did you see her? I only heard about it from Mary because her Stephen served at breakfast.'

'Because I changed the bed,' Tessa snapped. 'Twenty damn mattresses; Eliza couldn't manage all that linen on her own, so they sent me up. I was on my way out the chamber, peering over a pile of bedding when I saw her slowly making her way down. Her face was twisted in pain and she was biting her lip to stop from whimpering. And the Prince was there, with the Queen, waiting at the bottom of the stairs. Watching, to see if she had Passed. He had both hands in his pockets and that little smirk and he watched her all the way down. Every step. He never said a word nor moved to help.'

'Breeding,' Myrtle sneered. Tessa snorted.

'Well you can keep it.'

With the Test passed the kingdom was saved. The prince took her as his bride and they had a real princess at last, from a powerful dynasty, a union that strengthened their own kingdom. The couple were married three weeks later at the start of September. Every servant was ordered to wash and turn out to throw the pink and blue flowers. There was substantial largesse in the celebration. A feast was even put on for the servants; a fiddler was brought from the next valley, and there was dancing. Myrtle remembered the fiddler very well.

But not so well as they all remembered the couple walking out into the palace courtyard after the ceremony. The Prince in his finery, his black hair curling just a little above his collar. His cloying, exotic scent of bergamot masking the sweat of the warm day as he walked amid the flowered arches held by the double line of his cheering subjects. His long, straight nose that curled his upper lip as he smiled right and left right over his bride's head and the desire was savage in his eyes. And his bride, squinting in the bright sunlight, kept her eyes down; taking short breaths and chewing her lip as she controlled her pain in her slow walk half a pace behind. Holding her grace, hiding her limp. And spreading upwards from the low cut of her bodice, staining her pearl white skin was the blue and black blush of bruises that in three weeks, had not faded.

Autumn. There were subsidies for trade, prosperity came to the kingdom. The washerwomen felt it in the price of flour and fish. More ribbon at market. More pennies to buy it. There were reinforcements at the border, and peace, of a kind, sustained until winter. But still no heir.

That first infliction, the black flush after the storm-soaked August night, was only the start. Conceiving the heir was next. Then finally, whispers of a pregnancy at the start of Advent. A God-given Christmas gift for the Kingdom! Then at the end of January the washerwomen found the bright red political disaster smeared all over the bedsheets and a cloud fell over the palace.

The older woman washed that first sheet herself, taking her time, learning every spot and matching it to her memory, never contaminating the splashes from the tub's soap with those from her own eyes. Washerwomen: cleaning to purify the ugliness from the world. Then a storm shook the Kingdom one night in February. Without all was thunder and the screaming wind, beating the rain relentlessly against the stone walls, and within the Prince was beating the barren Princess against the chamber walls in fury. Still no heir, no heir and the wolf of the border kingdoms sniffing instability at the door, waiting, watching. Arming.

Three servants attended the Princess that night to bathe her skin and press it softly with witch hazel. But skin is not like the sheets the washerwomen took. While blood can be rinsed away, the blue blush cannot. The Prince was subdued in the days after this and the Princess kept to her chamber. The moon waxed and then when the washerwomen cleaned the menses off the sheets, blood from a battered face began appearing regularly.

'It's done,' Tessa said at last. She threw an end to Myrtle and they began twisting from both ends to ring out the water.

'It's all we can do,' the older woman sighed.

'We're hiding his crimes.'

'It's all we can do.'

'Can't she ask for help?' Myrtle blurted. 'Powerful family like hers, I'm sure they'd find this sort of carry-on not respectable.'

'Shame, I suppose,' the older woman answered.

'You had none,' Tessa reminded.

'Well,' the older woman's eyes darkened. 'Perhaps it's different asking a neighbour when you're in a spot of bother than a far-away Lord who's married you off.'

Tessa grinned and put her arm around the thin, hunched shoulders. 'Our little *coup de grace* was quite a triumph, wasn't it?'

'Yes,' the older woman admitted, allowing a half smile. 'Twenty-five years of drinking the rent, what was one more? He never knew what hit him.'

'Your poker, wasn't it?' Myrtle chuckled, digging Tessa in the ribs. 'And away he went at last! A well-co-ordinated operation!'

'Enough was enough.' The older woman leaned back from her waist and stretched out her shoulders. 'I make enough from the wash and now it's peaceful enough at home. I think it's different for you and your men these days. You build something. And your sons will be better. And your daughters will never have seen that sort of thing.' She eased out of the stretch and held out her arms. 'That's fine girls; bring it here now. It's the last, then we're done, and tomorrow is Sunday.'

'You seeing your fiddler tomorrow Myrtle?' Tessa asked with a devilish glint.

'Stop calling him that, his name's David.'

'He's good though, isn't he? At fiddling?'

'Stop it, Tessa. You spoil the poetry in everything. Tomorrow we'll walk up the crag to the tarn, and he will bring his violin.' Myrtle's eyes went misty, and her voice soft. 'I love it when he plays on the crag in the heather.'

'Are you still talking about the fiddle, Myrtle?'

'That's enough girls,' the older woman interrupted, 'pack it in and go home,' They emptied the tubs and splashed cold water on their faces to cool themselves, then dried off their arms and folded the last sheet. Myrtle opened the door to the bright, early May sun.

'How did your apple wine come off in the end?' she asked, turning hopefully to the old woman, who smiled knowingly.

'Well, I reckon it needs a test!' She stretched her arm through Myrtle's to support herself and reached for the other woman. 'You too Tess, come round to mine first and try it. If it's any good, you'll both have a jug. I'm sure you'd welcome some on your little outing tomorrow Myrtle, and Tess, I'm sure you and your husband aren't averse to a weekend tipple.'

The women walked home in the sunshine.

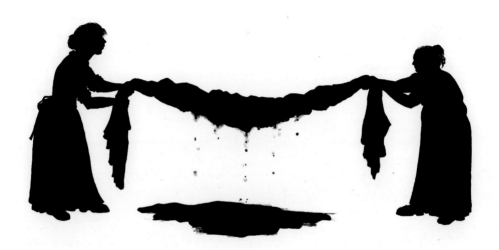

Sensitivity Scorned:
The Peasant and the Pea

A light is a sign. It should be read; heeded. Don't hide it under a bushel.

Throughout our times, and those before, we have been given many signs. A leveret killed by a fox with its corpse smeared along the path. The way crows gather in black clouds. Owls hawking eagles. All these auspices we read in the sky and earth; we have learned to look for them, to watch the colour of sunset, to count the families of magpies and interpret. We know how long to season oak, harden beech, the proportions to mix nettle and primrose. You ignore the sign readers at your peril.

When I was a young girl, my mother taught me how to read the signs. The first spring we sat together under the ash, the air was sweet and soft as cowslips and Queen Anne's lace made us a bright cushion. She taught me the repeated call of the song thrush, showed me the badger sets and how to hear of things to come in their snuffling; and in the call of owls, the movement of bats; the way moonlight falls in the secret places of deer.

With this meticulous looking and listening, I learned to love every contoured, coloured space of my country.

When I was a young woman, I plaited blossom in my hair and danced between the apple trees to wed a sweet boy. That night, before we bed, I slipped out in the full moonlight and buried a hard, dry pea in the earth where two paths crossed. I sprinkled water over it and whispered. The owl screamed thrice, and the earth shifted as a shoot broke through. Satisfied, I went back to my lavender scattered linen and my sweet Hrafn. I was pregnant by the end of the week.

I had a time with that carrying. As autumn came, I read omens in my aching breasts, thickening hair, painful hips and sickness. The baby growing in me never seemed still. When I read the skies to see rain coming, it writhed, it flopped over before high winds. One night, as lightning flashed, I awoke to a painless damp; blood streaked the sheets, and I roused my husband with shrieking fears. My mother was sent for and we three cleaned the linen and me, trying to read what it meant amid our tears. Two hours later, my heart leapt to feel it move again. But relief was broken by neighbours thundering at the door, screaming that a fire had broken out from the dry lightning storm and the barn was aflame. It had taken hold and the village lost four new-born calves. Hrafn ran off to help while my mother and I looked at each other in the fire's red glow. We read that sign; clear as morning.

That this child would not need to *learn* how to read them.

* * * *

When my daughter was born, she slithered into the world with her eyes wide open. Her left eye wandered outwards, unfocused, and the right was sharp and piercing; it fixed me as I took her to the breast. We named her Arndis and my mother mopped the child's skin with fennel and cinnamon water and blessed her with ashes. All the while, that unfocused left eye stayed open. I watched it that night, the second, and the third. It never focused. But after watching and reading, I knew; I could see it; I knew that eye could see beyond the signs I would ever read.

* * * *

When she is five, I take my daughter to the flower meadow. I teach her the names of flowers, which tree bark heals, the mood of the weather in a bird's cry. I teach her in the May morning to read the signs and she forgets nothing. She looks off into the distance and her wandering eye, blank behind the black pupil stares away left.

'Mother,' she beams at me. 'Harvest will be rich this year.'

I smile at her childish tones. But I'm proud.

'You read the signs well, little bird.'

But now she fixes me a serious look and her left eye droops more. I am suffocated by a sudden heavy gloom.

'Store it mother,' she pleads. 'And next harvest, and the one after that, and the next. Eke it out and plait straw for trading.'

'What, child?' I whisper.

'Famine mother,' she answers. 'In four years.' And she lays her light curled head on my lap and weeps.

This I could not read. But she could see it.

* * * *

Arndis turned nine with the last of the lambing. She was right. That summer was cold and damp, the valley crops were water-logged and most failed. Harvest came, and despite our blessing customs, we had little gathered at the thanking festival. Yet we were thankful. Our people trust their sign readers, and when I called for prudence with the plenty, it had been stored and extra planted. We survived. My child was hailed our greatest sign reader and thanked by those who came out of the forest and down from the foothills in need over winter. We fed them, cared for them in sickness, and weathered the famine through the last of the hunger months, until the first shoots of spring cabbage swelled for picking. In the

May, we drank our ale, gorged our bellies, and crowned Arndis with flowers as May queen. We danced amid the apple blossom and gave thanks in the warm sun that Beltane: famine was over at last.

* * * *

My child grew. We had no more children, but my sisters did, and my daughter led her cousins by the hand to the ash tree in the wildflowered meadow to teach them how to read the signs. She knew her gift but kept her teaching temperate. All our people in the valley and hills and woods loved her, our sacred light.

One morning, when she was fourteen, she awoke me early with her face creased in pain. As I rose to comfort her, I saw the skin beneath her ribs flushed blue with bruising that flowered there. I held her shaking shoulders as she cried in the grey dawn light.

'What happened?'

'There is something in the bed, mother, that hurts me. Like fingers piercing me, bone-like, evil; I've not slept all night but rolled on bones.'

We searched the bed. We pulled the blankets off to inspect the sheet. Finding nothing, we lifted the mattress, the bed itself. Still bewildered, I begged her to lie upon the bed again to try and show us where it dug the most; and her cries of pain were the wails of a lost child and it broke my heart so that I ripped the mattress to shreds for hurting her. Despairing, in a pile of feathers and straw we sat staring at the floor wondering what could have broken so violently the sleep of my child.

'Mother, that crack on the ground,' Arndis started to her feet. 'Look! It was never there before. When I kept my corn dolls under the bed for sweet dreams, it was never there before!'

I dug with my hands. I followed the crease, digging through the earthen floor. I called to my husband for a spade, we dug an appalling hole in the floor of the room while Arndis leaned over, scooping earth away and pleading that we persevere, it was near, nearer, close now.

A metre down, my daughter pulled out a shrivelled, mouldering pea.

'It was that?' Hrafn exclaimed. She looked at him, tears in her eyes.

'It is a sign,' she said, kneeling back on her heels, staring at the pea in her nightgown lap.

'What do you see, love?' She looked up at us again, frightened.

'Call everyone,' she murmured. 'Everyone. It is a sign, and we can't prevent this on our own.'

We called our people together in the long barn. I had seen my people dance at Thanking Festival here, and on Wassail; the Solstice tree clash in the trembling gold of the fire, vibrating the ceiling beams with their songs. This morning was tense. The elderly settled nearest the fire, folding their grandchildren in their laps and others squeezed around them knocking snow off their boots. We sign readers stood at the front, my daughter ahead. My mother, her silver hair cloaking her back, spoke first.

'You know my grandchild has proven her powers.' She paused to look at the stern faces ahead that twitched in nods. 'She has in her birth, her visions and warnings. She has kept us safe and prosperous.' Murmurs through the fire smoke. 'She warns us now.' Here she turned to my daughter. 'Speak child. Tell them.'

Arndis stood forward. From behind I could only see her long hair, darkened to light brown from its childish gold. Her shoulders were thin; she was always a small girl. But her back which faced me was firm, her voice when she spoke, though low, never wavered and I bit my lip to crush the emotion threatening to dismay me. My child. So young and holding the thick weight of our future in her thin arms that should hold the blessings of flowers and herbs.

'There will be disease,' she said. 'It is even now festering in the ground, coursing under the warrens of our land and souring the soil. Crops will die and then disease will spread to us and all, from the smallest field poppy to the greatest boar in the forest, all will die.'

I watched the people's faces as cold, bony fear clutched their hearts and stopped their breathing. Silence followed.

'Can it be stopped?'

Arndis sought the voice with her eyes. 'Yes. It is the war our King is fighting on his further borderlands. The dead, the starvation and the rot have infected those lands beneath the fields. It is spreading fast. But,' and here she seemed to steel herself, 'If I can gain an interview with him and put forward an application for peace, we could arrest the chaos.'

My mother twisted to her granddaughter, steel hair falling over her shoulder. Her voice hissed. 'You surely don't bid to make this journey?'

'It's my duty, grandmother. I must.'

I did not see how my mother swallowed hard, her eyes wild and her hands before her face. I saw nothing but my own child's head as I screamed protests and clutched those thin shoulders tight to me.

* * * *

I watched my daughter climb into her saddle. She had to jump a little to make the distance to the stirrup because she is still so young, and she shuffled awkwardly, and I cried then for how will she convince a king if she can barely reach her own reins? I pinned mistletoe to her bridle for luck and stood back. My husband urged his horse on after her, his heart soothed to go with his daughter. My own heart was cracking. I saw the fear through her brave smile, and I could not speak, but squeezed her calf muscle as she moved off. A five-day journey across the mountain pass and down the plains through the late winter snow.

I was restless all week. I read the winds, the way the wolves came closer at night. I watched twelve crows descend in a ring and squawk, fighting over a dead vole. Another snow fall mixed the mud-stained melt and the paths between our village homes became stiff ridges to snap an ankle on. Grey fog descended, hiding the valley's peaks and trees, and hung there for three turns of the moon. The weeks stretched out. Eventually, I saw two magpies bickering on the nearest branch of the willow row on my way to the wood pile one morning. The sky had cleared, and I knew my daughter was coming home.

Two more moons I waited at the meadow edge to look out for her. At last, as the sun turned the afternoon sky purple and gold, I saw two figures on horseback. Hitching my skirts under my arm like a wash bundle, I raced through the muddy snow towards them.

* * * *

It had not gone well. By the fire, with my mother, my pale daughter told us of her petition. Of how the king had laughed and put my husband in chains and made him watch the derision of our child. How the duke demanded she prove her power, and took her to a room with seven beds, each piled with twenty mattresses, and bade her lay down on each to find the old pea hidden under one of them. How the prince had leered as she lay. Here she paused. Hrafn took her hand and finished; they were lucky they were not whipped for presumption on foreign policy, and they were sent away. We passed the hot ale around in silence.

'What now?' I asked.

My daughter stared at the fire.

'Be frugal with what we take from the land,' she said. 'Give back a morsel of all we take. Then when we have nothing, we'll have a fat stag at the door. Keep clean. And dance and sing because we'll need our spirits. We must love our land and each other to balance the hate of that king.'

* * * *

We watched the deer that rutting. We left offerings. We blessed the spring when it came, cautiously, and saw the birth of our lambs, of fallow deer, of pheasants. We lived carefully, with a new look between each other, of a shared, unspoken thing. When summer came, we danced the solstice in, our shouts to drown the news from the boarder that disease crept closer, emptying villages, and laying families waste. That summer we had no rain, and at Lammas, our wheat was meagre. Disease was spreading up the mountainside and while the sun shone pitilessly, we could feel the earth dying. Green summer browned and cattle grew thin. More came from the hills for our decoctions and infusions against plague.

And then winter. I watched the sun swell the thick, blood red of the Ragnarok stories, the poisoned red light that drives men mad. We drew in our breath, tensed. The earth was the steel death of winter and it dragged on past Imbolc and on towards Beltane, still with the low blood sun over short days. We continued our offerings. We tended the few weak lambs that crept, mewling, into life. There was only brown dead grass for them to eat in this eternal winter where the green fingers of spring had failed to stretch out from underground. Would we just die with our land? And then the falcons began circling high above the mountain and I read the horses beneath on the mountain pass. They showed me the death might be a different kind as the king's soldiers approached our village.

Disease had spread in the city and Famine clawed at the keep's walls. The prince had died. The king had realised the power of my daughter and in his anger and shame, he named us cursed witches. He ordered our capture and the soldiers had come for us.

The sign readers stepped forward. We were bound in chains and thrust into a cart and borne away. The light was hidden from our people.

* * * *

A light is a sign. Arndis made a light. It was hard for me was to trust what she saw; what I had never seen. Our arrival to the keep was a humiliation we had never known. The city's populace, scabbed with sores, festering black and red with plague had turned out to jeer the witches. They threw what rotten vegetables were left in that starving place and I cringed to see my mother's back sag, her silver hair smeared with filth. Hate is a weapon and they hated us. And watching them mock my child, and cow my proud mother, I hated them too. But Arndis leaned forward, trying to clasp hands of the mob and press remedies in their fists. We have healed plague in our home, and as they threw the shit of their animals at her, she spoke calmly: yarrow infusion for fever; garlic and wild thyme against infection. Even chained to a dungeon pillar later, I felt relief that we were shielded from the vicious hate that had been whipped up in these people.

We waited there three moons. My mother and we three daughters watched the star and moon patterns through the small grating and tried to balance the good and evil we saw there. But Arndis looked at nothing, only leaned back against her pillar and idly fondled the fetters. Then on the third evening, we were visited by the Duke. When he swept into the room, I watched my daughter flinch and shrink back into the shadows. The Duke of the bedchamber and one hundred and forty mattresses to lay my child upon. My mother and sisters and I stepped forwards, our shoulders a wide wall in front of Arndis as he leered.

My mother lifted her chin. 'Well?'

'You will be executed at dawn,' the duke said, an ugly scorn cutting his nose and mouth.

'To give hope to your people? Now you understand the importance symbols?' my mother sneered.

The duke leaned in, his face close enough for me to spit at. 'You will be burned,' he smiled. 'That should cleanse the evil.'

'And the war?' asked one of my sisters. 'If that continues, burning us will make no difference.'

'It will feed the revenge of the king to watch you writhe,' the duke snapped, turning to her. We stood in our walled line, our faces stone, staring forwards with our chins up and our shoulders touching. We must not break. My mother inclined her head in assent.

'Good luck with it,' I said. 'You know we are all lost. Our deaths will at least be more painless.' I felt my daughter move behind me, my child of sixteen with a life stolen from her and my rage flamed. And in my rage, I read a comforting vision. 'You too, will suffer a death of fire, sir,' I cursed. 'It will consume you as you stand and catch your hair and fine robe in a living pillar of flame. Your skin will crisp and crackle like a Yule hog and your last long seconds will be anguish and horror. You will fall to skinless knees and beg for death, but your voice will be choked in smoke, and all will flee from you. I curse you, sir.'

He hit me. He wore an amethyst on his knuckle that burst into my cheek and eye with the crack of bone and dull suck of flesh. But from our stone wall of shoulders, I did not even reel back, but was motionless, standing masonry. Blood came from my eyebrow and I smiled. He looked at us in confusion and growing horror while he nursed his useless fist, then swept from the room.

That night, we slept little. I held Arndis to me as my mother clutched her daughters round her. We sang to spur our defiance and watched the moon, swollen and silver. We wrung love from our last hours together and tried to rejoice through our strained wakefulness, that we were together at least. Three generations of sign readers. A pattern. A sign itself.

And then the last sign came. Just as night was almost at odds with morning, a noise from the window roused us. A magpie had landed there and strutted back and forth in its tailored waistcoat and frock coat. We watched it, till it was joined by another. Then another and another. We read aghast, the swelling visitation until the seventh arrived. It held a piece of sweet-pea in its beak – the pink and purple of late June. We stared at each other. Arndis spoke.

'Can't you see it now mother, when it is so near?'

I looked at her. Those thin shoulders, her long hair; her heart that loved so blithely. My heart broke again. I saw her, our light, and I saw now what the signs said. My mother saw it, and my sisters and my nieces as we stared, dismayed at Arndis, with the eye that never met ours, but saw further.

'When I shout run,' she whispered, 'do not hesitate.'

* * * *

The rest is a series of dark pictures. We were pulled out at dawn; to the roars of more jeering. We cried now and the king and duke laughed. But the cramping, biting, wrenching loss was not for our own lives, but my child's, who knew, all along, what her fate was.

We were bound to stakes and hefted onto pyres. The man in the black mask with his burning brand stood by. My breath caught and my heart fluttered like a wren and the damp on my hands and under my arms made my bonds slip. The king was speaking but I heard nothing through the black buzz of 'witches!' as the executioner held up his brand and walked towards my child. Only a child. And such fear of a child. She twisted her head towards me and smiled, beautifully. It was serene, joyful, and it smeared through my tears into something misty and permanent. I could see her mouth the words 'now, mother!' like a triumphant shout, as if she was starting a race, not her death, and the pyre was lit and the faggots caught and then something glorious came from my child, a light, a white shimmering light, of which magic she was made, erupted; burst like a waterfall and fanned out in a summer heat we had not felt for ten months.

Our bonds singed first, and we slipped into the kindling. We waded through it, and gathering wrists of sister, mother and child, we ran through the crowd, ran through the gates as soldiers bolted past us with pails for the explosion. We ran out of that cursed place as it was engulfed in the flaming inferno of my child; burning duke, King and pauper; melting metal, boiling lead, scorching septic earth and slaughtering the pestilence, war and corruption that infected the land.

A light is a sign. Her light could not be hidden.

* * * *

In some lands, burning cleanses. It opens space for light, it enriches the soil. The trees grow stronger and the regrowth is thicker; birds return. My daughter's fire did this for our land. We made the journey back through forest and mountain pass, while the iridescent blue of kingfishers darted past us in forest streams and magpies called. As we reached the willows at the edge of our home, we saw the purple and gold of crocuses had broken through the earth. Spring had come and our land lived again.

* * * *

I am much older now, but I am a favourite with my sisters' grandchildren. My hair is a steel cloak down my back and my husband's is a long white cape. I keep a small, shrivelled pea on my hearth to show these babies and tell them about our greatest sign reader, as I teach them to read the meaning of magpies, what will come from the colour of sunsets and how to make a decoction from oak bark.

And the light is returned to our people.

Oversensitive

Once there was a young princess who was taught that grace, charm, and beauty were the only qualities she would ever need. Taking this as read, she grew up with the physical poise of a prima donna, the perfectly accentuated cheek bones of a Renaissance model, and was astoundingly, utterly stupid.

This didn't worry her father as he was very proud of his daughter's beauty. He enjoyed being able to show her off to his courtiers and she would win them all with pretty smiles and pretty – though short, comments. What her mother thought, we'll never know, as she was not asked.

And so the young girl grew to the trembling precipice of womanhood (somewhere between the age of seven and sixteen depending on the perversity of social, historical and cultural conventions) sheltered behind the castle walls. She took her exercise in the manicured and well dusted gardens, hung with laburnum and lilac but no bees – they unnerved her – and deer and rabbits would gently patter between the lawns and never shit anywhere. On days of bad weather, she walked the long gallery hung with enormous portraits of her beautiful ancestors who had reached the pinnacle of princess-hood – perfect stillness, so their graceful beauty can be admired free from interruption of human emotion. This way she could take her exercise and her dress would never be spoiled and those pretty curls that hung at her nape so deliciously always kept their shape.

She never jumped in puddles like you or I, or climbed trees to explore the secret world of birds. She never rolled down hills in a dizzy giggle or ran with other children to feel what the wind is like on your face and hair. She never tested her strength on bars to see if she could save herself if she fell out of a window or read books for hours to dream of far-off worlds she would one day ride her horse to when she was grown. She never learned how to make ceramic bottles or cakes, or patterned glass, or asked why the sky is blue or how it rains, or what makes marble statues in underground caves or who wrote poems so beautifully they made you weep.

Instead, she learned how to turn her head and look up through her lashes prettily, she cried if a bee came near her and she was terrified of dogs. She never lounged disgracefully in an armchair, but sat neatly upright, thus often got back ache.

And now, at the cusp of womanhood, she was ready to marry. A charming young prince was found from a Kingdom of the Middle Lands. His parents were the Heath King and Queen, the crown to which young Prince Reuben would ascend when he came of age.

The prince was an accomplished young man. He was a joyful and buoyant soul in the way a body will be after a childhood of jumping in puddles, racing his mother on horseback and learning to cook the perfect Dauphinois potato with his father. He had all the sacrificial pity for the poor of an Oscar Wilde Christ metaphor, and he charmed whole armies with his beautiful singing voice. He was very sought after.

He was excited about marriage. He longed to knit his soul with another being and forge a new age, hand in hand with her. He had had certain uncertain flutterings, which his mother had explained to him at length when he was young; even though it made him blush terribly, but the princess was certainly beautiful and at least now he felt like he had a fair idea of how to Proceed. But first! He longed to become intimate with her sweet charms, learn the musical notes of her voice and be lost in them as they talked (so he imagined, dreaming indulgently on his silken draped balcony) late into the moonlight. He was overcome with the thought of the romance.

The princess was duly brought, in all pomp, to the court of the Heath King.

All the court were captivated by the princess' beauty. She certainly knew how to twirl her curls adorably – it made you quite lose track of what she was saying. The prince spent three days sat in her company by the shady lake of his palace on a tasselled golden quilt, lost in her face.

They talked. Well, he talked. He told her all his plans for his kingdom, how to modernise, how to raise the standard of living, how to develop and beautify. She smiled gratifyingly and agreed. The prince lay with his head in her lap while she stroked his long hair and felt very happy. He pushed down the strange uncertainty that he felt that even after several weeks, he couldn't say he knew her very well.

One day, the queen declared a picnic. They would ride over to the Maypole green to sport themselves. The queen was an excellent horsewoman. Kin were invited, dogs were gathered, but the expression on the princess' face was stricken with horror.

The family were aghast to learn that she could not ride, she was scared of dogs, she preferred not to be in the sun too long and found it troubling to eat off her lap. The king grimaced and the queen exchanged looks with the dowager duchess, her sister. A conference was held, carriages, substantial furniture and tents were brought. The picnic would go ahead.

Installed gracefully on a hastily constructed dais, the princess arranged her skirts gorgeously around her and smiled. Entertainments were brought. The prince and his father regaled the company with a charming duet. The queen talked vehemently on sustainable forestry policy and made many jokes. The prince's little sister showed her acrobatic skills and laughed merrily as she stood on her horse's back in canter. The dowager aunt lowered the tone with a bawdy song. The princess was asked for a song or recitation, but she demurely professed her ignorance. All were gay and the royal family applied themselves to getting to know the young princess; asking her questions and her opinion on all number of things, to which she mostly lowered her eyes and smiled prettily.

After a while, a breeze sprung up, the princess complained of a draught, was in horror of ants and strenuously felt her gown was an inappropriate colour for the approaching evening. Under such duress, the court retired to the civility of buildings.

Now the dowager aunt was a canny old woman, and she could guess the queen's thoughts with unfailing success. She summoned her for conference that evening.

'The thing is,' she began, after shutting firm the door, 'the girl is indeed very pretty, very charming and very graceful, but she's utterly stupid and unforgivably dull.'

The queen sunk into a chair and sighed. 'I fear you're right.'

'We must summon your son,' the duchess asserted, 'talk some sense into him.'

The queen bridled at this most bad temperedly. 'My son is not stupid,' she snapped. 'He's got a brain, he'll see this soon enough.'

'I don't dispute it,' assured the duchess. 'But he is ensnared in the first flame of attraction which we must temper with a dousing of patience. Allow them to be daily in each other's company. But let's have plenty of other company here too, and no talk of marriage for a year. It'll soon run its course.'

The queen nodded. 'Yes. Let's get him here and tell him we'll arrange the marriage for next May to give them time to plan their life thereafter.'

Prince Reuben was summoned. His love was enquired after. His mother and aunt were sweet and patient as he poured out to them his ardent admiration.

'Time is sweet for young lovers!' smiled his aunt.

'You both must enjoy it!' laughed his mother. 'We shall all enjoy our time together, sweetly, each day unrestrained. Give us time to plan the most splendid wedding and arrange your quarters. It'll all be ready within the year!'

Prince Reuben frowned at this. 'A year?'

'What's the rush?' his mother cried. 'your time together is not fettered. Get to know each other. Travel together! Do things! So that your loves may by day increase. Just give us time to build a palace fit for a princess!'

41

Reuben felt in his heart they were right and that uncertain feeling he tried to ignore would disperse as they knew each other better. He assented and ran off to find his princess, who was at that point weeping loudly as a storm had begun and the thunder frightened her.

The queen and her sister watched him go, racing to the wailing source away in the long gallery.

'I don't know if *I* can stick her a whole year,' the queen grimaced.

The duchess shook her head and fervently grasped her sister's hand. 'Nor I.'

****

After serious reflection, the queen and duchess thought it ungenerous to write the girl off altogether, and instead set about attempting to Improve her Character. Thus, the royal court did what it could to educate, embolden and enliven the beautiful, graceful and charming princess till they were quite blue in the collective face with it. In the end, some bad parenting just can't be undone.

One desperate night, Prince Reuben threw himself at his mother's feet in her chamber and wept. She rested her hands on his dark head as he poured out his woe.

'I had just hoped we'd have something in common!' he wailed. 'And she just won't try new things! I suggested we both try archery, she thoroughly baulked and fretted about the soft skin on her hands. I suggested exploring the forest and camping out – too dirty, I suggested mountains – too high; her complexion does badly when out of breath, I suggested sailing – too wet. I asked what she would like to do, and she said she didn't know! If she only had … some opinions!'

'Well,' chastised his mother, 'she's not the outdoors type. What about indoor things?'

'I suggested baking, she said boring, I said music – too hard; reading – the concentration gives her wrinkles. It's a disaster mother! How can I honourably extricate myself?'

His mother smiled to herself. 'There is a way.'

****

The next evening the queen and duchess summoned the princess. They sat her down comfortably, closed the window against the draught and gave her sweet wine. When she was comfortable, the queen tentatively began.

'My dear, we have a custom here. It is something we must do before you marry my son.'

The princess looked afraid and her lip began to quiver.

42

'No no!' the queen hastily consoled, clutching at the young girl's hand, while her sister turned away, rolling her eyes. 'It is nothing terrible – don't be afraid! It is merely a custom that twelve weeks before the wedding, the princess must sleep in a bed of twenty mattresses. It is proof to all the land that you are a real princess.'

Here the princess looked fit to wobble again.

'It's really nothing more than a custom! There's no harm in it!' the queen urged while the dowager ferociously studied the tapestries. The princess at last desisted snivelling and agreed to sleep in the High Bed that very night.

****

The queen wedged the old dry pea under the bottom mattress hefted up by the duchess with many a grunt of exertion.

'I feel like a ruthless bitch,' she sighed.

'They'll make each other miserable for years,' the duchess retorted. 'That's worse.'

****

The following morning the princess stormed into breakfast, limping gracefully, in floods of tears. She declared she had been tricked and deceived by this heartless kingdom and was returning home at once. She had slept dreadfully and eventually got up and dismantled the bed and found the pea that had kept her awake all night. She summoned a carriage and left that morning.

The prince sighed. 'Oversensitive,' he murmured.

****

In the end, the prince found a princess who spoke three languages, and enjoyed high speed skiing that frankly horrified him, but he was willing to give it a go. They lived happily ever after.

And the beautiful graceful, charming princess? I feel I have been unkind to her. After all, it wasn't all her fault. Well, she married; indeed, a strong handsome, brave prince who was often out hunting and would happily return home to lay his head in his lover's silent, smiling lap and tell her all about it. They were very well suited. They even had a daughter, who they hoped one day, would be beautiful, graceful and charming. And as a little chubby three years old child, she was charming and would make her mother laugh at her childish games. They would walk together in the palace gardens, and even once, before she could be stopped, the little princess broke free from her mother's hand in glee and ran straight through a puddle, splashing mud all over her silk gown. The young queen shrieked in dismay.

Then she threw back her head, and laughed.

The Twelve Dancing Princesses

Forests hide secrets. Be not beguiled by the innocence of primroses and gold star flowers and cowslips. Trees harbour secrets. Beneath the trees of this land are the smothered mountains. Valleys tip their rocks down into shards and slivers of rivers and it is cold up here much of the year. Unscaleable summits glitter silver and diamond in the snowy sunlight that fails to penetrate the deepest valleys.

Mountains divide.

There is a softer valley among these forbidden frowning mountains where the emerald hills slope gently down and graze sheep. The river gathers its tributaries and bloats, glutted. Dwellings now emerge behind slopes. These knot together towards a grand stone fortress that shimmers in the hazy trapped heat that fattens the grapes on the receding ascending vines.

We have reached the centre, the naval of the world. The crux of these events.

After a night more than usually opioid in fragrance and the stupor of warmth, the king awoke in his castle in the valley. His dreams had been haunted with the memory of his lost queen, a smooth, lithe girl; too young some had said. But after the first glow of her beauty had lost its novelty as child after child was born with no son, he became angry. His frustration led to cruelty, then ferocity to his queen and daughters. He awoke on this morning with the condemning face of his eldest daughter piercing his dreams and that disgust at the memory of his young wife vanishing to the forest. Yet the King was accustomed to his power safely enveloped in the valley and did not like to be foiled. So on awakening on this morning, the King's first instinct was perturbation. As tendrils of pine scent insinuated through the open window, the King sought for the lingering cause of his unease; and remembered.

His daughters' shoes.

Seized with apprehension, the King sprung from his sumptuous silken bed hung with flowers; dashed from the raised dais of his sleeping throne and billowed through the royal doorway, his brocaded bed robes rippling softly over the floor.

Unceremoniously, despite the best efforts of alert and powdered footmen, the king burst violently into the bedroom of the royal Princesses. Not a glance gave he their twelve velvet curtained beds, but his gaze fell hungrily on the floor running against the wall. Here in a row were twelve pairs of hand sewn silken slippers. They lay in useless scraps of brilliant coloured tatters, disgorged like ripped and silken entrails.

For twelve days now the King had found it necessary to replace his daughters' shoes. And for twelve days not one of his daughters would explain what had destroyed them. This insubordination sat ill with the King's disposition.

The screams of fury and fear echoed through the valley from the castle and ricocheted off the bare peaks for some time after a brooding silence had once more taken hold of the castle.

****

The mountains divide. Kingdoms nestled in those valleys are riven asunder by knife point crags, cutting each off from the others at the throat. Negotiating the thinning paths fraught with scree, blocked by reproachful stones to reach each purified summit was legendary with danger. There had been many deaths of travellers reported by the herders, cut off by mists or storms, who either perished of cold on the mountain face or marched smartly off a precipice. The people of these kingdoms were safe from invasion. News rarely came.

Therefore, when the King desired to advertise for assistance in the matter of his daughters' shoes, he feared limited success. After long state discussions with royal advisors bustling to and fro through the airy corridors of the castle, the King agreed the reward must be substantial. Whichever man of his own lands or others could discover what his reticent daughters did with their shoes each night would have the pick of them; a Duchy; the store of ancient amethysts and finally, in time, the throne itself. But if he should fail, the King decreed he may never marry elsewhere; blighting his own dynasty forever.

They came in droves.

The Kingdom was nearly doubled in population. Emergency stores of wheat were dragged open. The year's supply of wine was carried by the gallon to the Royal table in celebration of the valiant guests. Sheep were scared off and lost by the tide of men pouring over the mountain ridges; orchards were plundered by exhausted travellers. The Kingdom was saved from being overrun only by the sword point of the mountains that pierced and murdered many more with cold. The bodies of golden princes; their russet mantles ragged and their beautiful faces disfigured with pain, were carried down when the weather cleared. The Princesses sighed over the waste of these flowers of their clans while competitors rejoiced.

It went on. The spring heightened and blossoms burst, then browned. Each prince or young nobleman was celebrated and feasted on arrival. Then, against custom and discretion, the young man was prepared a small cot in the bedchamber of the princesses. He resided without while they readied for bed, then was summoned by a gentlewoman. The twelve Princesses, each sweet face restful with their long hair coiled and cascading from the pillow, slept. The Prince was to keep watch during the balmy night and report to the King their movements. And each morning the Prince would start awake to find the Princesses staring disdainfully at him from their cushioned beds; he would raise in horror to behold the neat row of ruined slippers and be banished from the Castle by the furious King.

The Kingdom's supplies ran low. One young nobleman after another was ruined. The King despaired.

****

Green leaves now shone gold and blood red in the evening sunlight. Harvest at last, replenishing the Kingdom's squandered stocks. The King's subjects rallied themselves after a summer of starvation and began bringing their herds in. The balmy air became crisper and the higher peaks enclosing the valley heaped up with snow.

One afternoon a young goat herder of that Kingdom descended from the hillside. He was fed on the milk and honey of that country and grew tall on its wine and meat. He was a handsome youth, strong with climbing after his flock, with blue eyes that sparkled with the distant mountains and his russet hair, recalling the red and brown leaves of the forest below fell in soft curls around his face.

He was preoccupied as he left the bare hillside for the forest. Dissatisfied. It was the news of every village in the Kingdom that the King was still evaded by his daughters' secret. The youth was not surprised. He had seen many of these Princes flounder on the mountains, nay, carried them down too. As he helped lay out the beautiful corpses, their naïve faces untouched by care he felt almost resentment. They were weak. They were unworthy of his country. Why should the fertile land go to glut the Kingdom of another who would fortify their own lands with its wealth, then leave the hillsides to rot? All for these soft, pale youths. It was with these thoughts that the young goat herder reached the thickening trees of evergreen and ash and birch.

The first leaf fell outside the casement of the Princesses' chamber.

Ambling between the trees, the youth paused. He had reached the deciduous door of the copse. This part of the forest stretched in all directions and the youth always stopped himself here, impressed with its closeness; its stillness. Wind never penetrated, and the only noise was of soft slow crows flapping lugubriously between trees close by. Forests hide secrets. The youth never felt it more so than now, with the melancholy red light stretching itself out between the silent trees and an unexpected mist that wreathed and laced itself in fine patterns around the trunks.

Breathlessly enthralled by the misty solitude, the youth was shocked from his reverie by a twig snap behind him. A crow like croak of a greeting and a wizened old woman stepped from behind a tree. She had the look of a fortune teller from her stiff, faded garments and basket of ribbands and trinkets. He greeted her, yet she ignored pleasantries and spoke only:

"I know what your heart desires. I will help."

Our hero was under her spell. At once enchanted he was drunk with thought – the overwhelming love of his mountain pointed country; the bitterness of it being ruined by the acquisitioning of strangers; the jealousy of these weak pale men and even yet, desire for the Princesses, glimpsed hosting festivities in the villages, and each fair limb softer than the gentlest green hillock of the valley's plains; each hair lock coiled more intoxicatingly than the red vineyards ascending each hillside.

Our youth agreed.

"Take this cloak," the leathered woman said. "You will find it useful. And drink nothing the Princesses give you." The woman had a bright twinkle in her leaf-green eyes. The youth thanked her and turned to leave.

"One more thing," the young-old woman checked him. "Those girls are much cleverer than their father thinks. Respect that."

The goat herder nodded. He merely called at home to summarise his intentions to his father, then after washing himself in the cold, pine stream, he marched straight for the palace.

****

The kitchens were ablaze once more. Stuffed pheasants and quail eggs. Frozen shorts of grappa between portions of veal and wild boar bristling on the engraved silver. The Great Hall was glittering with a thousand candles against the encroaching darkness and the sharp autumn air that tumbled in from the mountains. Our young goat herder had never seen such cloth to adorn a table so woven with gold and coloured thread. Fragrant new wines washed down each rich mouthful.

The King sat disdainfully at the great table, six daughters at each side of him. Each was dressed in rich red material, the bodices delicately woven and lined with fur. Twelve pairs of eyes rested at times throughout the meal on the young man. The eldest three conferred in proud whispers, dubious of his rustic manner. The younger sisters looked at him with more pity. He was handsome, and they had seen so many handsome men wasted. The sixth daughter found him more refreshing. She was rather taken with his healthful air. Her twin was the other side of the King so she could not whisper her thoughts and light giggles, but she occasionally leaned back and caught her eye behind her father's metal-grey head. She surveyed the curly headed red lipped youth at length. He had caused a bit of a stir, refusing all food offered but ate his own bread and cheese from the Royal plate. He looked about himself in general, or occupied himself with his plate. He caught the sixth daughter's eye in one of his visual perambulations of the hall. To his surprise, she

48

smiled and winked at him. Taken aback, the goat herder stared. Then, gathering himself, he seized his goblet and raised it firmly to her with a broad white smile.

The King scowled.

****

The moon shone. The ritual began again. The small cot was brought forth to the daughters' chamber, and the young man summoned within when the Princesses were appropriately apparelled in their white night robes. He blinked at the sumptuous tapestries and velvet bed curtains, the white woven lace and flowers garlanding posts and pillars.

In his daze, the eldest sister approached holding a copper goblet. Her fingers were long and slender with sharp nails. He looked at her cold proud face as she offered him the cup.

"Drink." She said.

He took the cup and drained it. The sixth Princess flinched but avoided interrogating herself why. She was the first to lay her tumbling hair over her pillow. One by one the Princesses followed and drew their embroidered coverlets around them.

When the last candle had been extinguished, the goat herder leaned toward the wall by his low cot, and spat out the red liquid onto his pile of clothes so the spatter would make no noise.

The moon shone and silence reigned like a deity through the castle. The goat herder stared at the silver light shimmering against the wall. It had illuminated a tapestry depicting dancing women in a forest with harts and boar in an eerie light. Gazing transfixed in the monochrome shadows, the goat herder fancied they moved. In the still air he thought of the old legend of music emitted from the turning night stars. On a night glittering as brightly as this he fancied it would be louder, like the sound of a finger around a fine glass as he saw once at fayre. A glassy silvery sound he fancied he could hear like a bell; a signal as the tapestry figures twitched and swayed in the violet night.

A bell. The sound of silver, the colour of ringing glass, melting together. The goat herder heard a movement from the eldest sister's bed, the slithering of sheets ruched back. Tight fast shut he kept his own eyes. More sounds as each Princess rose and dressed in garments of gold and silver, pearl and light refracting, the colour of moonlit nights. They brushed their hair, metallic in the lustrous night and slipped one by one behind the tapestry of the dancing women in the forest, capering and laughing with the harts and boar.

There was silence. The youth in panic ripped the sheets back and sprang up – cloak in hand. Running to the tapestry barefoot he slung the rough mantle around

49

him over his under garments and followed through the newly revealed stone passage behind the tapestry.

****

The youth followed the sounds of laughter. The passage was draughty, and he was glad of the cloak. He hurried after them until the moonlit clad Princesses were in sight. The sixth Princess had fallen behind, pondering why the goat herder so scrupulously refused all palace refreshment, then drank back her sister's potion with such relish. On instinct she glanced back down the stone passage towards the distant bed chamber. The goat herder froze in terror, then gasped. He comprehended the use of his cloak as the fair face saw him not, and turned back towards her sisters.

****

Forests hide secrets. Dead and gone were the beguiling primroses in the blue winter night as the goat herder followed the twelve Princesses out of the stone passage and into the hillside forests. The youth recognised the still pines where they stopped, and once more felt their strangeness. Around him the moon threw sharp ink shadows; frost glimmered on the fallen pinecones and broken twigs. The air froze. The world was metal spikes and silver needles in the metal night; blue and silver, black and silver and the pearl light was so cold. The goat herder's feet were red and stiff under his cloak in that stillest, strangest part of the forest and his crystallised breath wreathed around his face as he reeled in the frozen night. Each Princess, moonlit clad, silver clad, pearl and diamond clad reeled in the knife edge night, dazed and entranced. As they stood, the stillness flickered. The trees flickered.

At once it felt less cold as a lace white mist crept in to caress each frozen twig with is moist fingers. All thirteen watched the smoky mist, as it silently swarmed the forest.

It cleared. The air was soft and inviting. The goat herder looked up to see in horror that the forest had at last given up its secret and transformed; throwing outward leaves of silver. Gone were the green pines and beautifully bedecked in silver were trees that glimmered. Brighter than the moonlight, colder than the stars, the twinkling leaves nodded softly in the breeze.

Enchanted, the beguiled goat herder touched the leaf above him. Then he ripped off a small branch and smothered it inside his cloak. Several sisters looked round at the crack that echoed through the still night. Seeing nothing, they walked on.

Following the Princesses, the youth crept on in the new warm air. The forest glittered ethereally and the path was easy in the silver light that fell like liquid in droplets between the trees. The watery beams played on the curls of the Princesses' transformed hair.

They walked on. But this was only the first of the forest's secrets as swiftly once more, the trees transformed into further finery. Now the cold silver light brightened and warmed, honeyed and thickened and the forest burst forth gold. Gold were the shining leaves glistening on the silky curls, gold was the air heaped up in the midnight forest and gold was the light that dripped in caramel and amber on the faces of the laughing Princesses. The Midas night was uplifting and the Princesses broke into a run. The gold rippled ahead of their tripping steps.

The goat herder broke another branch to conceal beneath his cloak. Again, the Princesses looked around at the crack, but seeing nothing, proceeded cautiously. The sixth Princess frowned and again slipped behind.

The next secret of the forest nearly betrayed the young goat herder entirely as an audible gasp escaped his lips. The forest was now bejewelled in fantastic diamonds. Each branch drooped heavily with resplendent fragments and the rich hangings swung pendulously in the soft breeze. Some diamonds hung like clustered precious berries, others stretched languorously into four points, but all caught the moonlight to throw down innumerable rainbows on every trunk, twig and inch of ground. The forest was at once a glinting prism, blinding with the aurora of diamonds.

The eldest Princess, transfigured with joy now that her haughty countenance was left languishing back at the castle, took up the jubilant cry of 'nearly there!' and all twelve Princesses ran on laughing together. Now when the youth broke a third branch to ensconce in his cloak, not one heard.

The forest was ripe with its final secrets. The group of nocturnal adventurers stopped at the shore of a silver lake with willows trailing their fingers in its ripples that reflected shimmering mirrors back on the branches. Awaiting the twelve Princesses were twelve boats, each manned by a young fair man dressed richly. As the Princesses jostled amid giggles and shouts to their boats and partners, the youth slipped in with the sixth Princess. They took off at such speed on the windless night that the Princess's hair whipped maddeningly in our youth's face and he had to crush himself against the stern. All the same, the extra weight made the boat sink lower in the water and he winced as he heard the Princess comment at how they were lagging behind.

The forest's final secret. On the far side of the lake yawned the mouth of a capacious cave, all a sparkle with light. As the goat herder followed the Princesses in blinking, he saw columns bedecked with fragrant garlands and twisted with silver leaves; stalactites dripping thousands of candles and stalagmites serving as tables; draped with fine cloth and loaded with sparkling goblets and fruits. But the goat herder knew not to touch the food at a fairy ball, though the Princesses fell upon them, as his mother years ago before she died had warned him in her hearthside tales of the pining sickness that falls on mortals on tasting fairy fruit.

Now such a dance sprang up that the goat herder was breathless just watching; indeed from dodging the dancers as they were flung towards him. Each of the twelve Princesses danced with her Prince who glowed supernaturally, softly, warmly with the light of the forest's secrets. They danced in pairs amidst the throng of other elven creatures, they danced in great lines up and down the hall altogether; sister clasped sister by the waist to spin dizzyingly; there was leaping and cheering and quaffing of wine as beaming sister and dancer grasped goblets high above them as they span and gulped between steps. They danced and drank and ate for hours; they covered themselves in slops of wine, laughing till our youth was fair pining to join in. They danced on as the full moon's reflection traversed the length of the lake at the mouth of the shimmering cave and descended in the West.

Suddenly the music abruptly stopped. The twelve Princesses looked down with resignation and following their eyes the youth noticed that after hours of dancing on the rough cave floor, their shoes were worn through to tatters.

Then began the most heart rending of farewells as Princess clutched elf to breast and smothered them in tearful embraces. Finally each dancing Princess scooped up her ruined slippers and fled barefoot to the boats.

Again the goat herder followed the sixth sister into her boat, having been smitten with her spirited dancing and jokes with her partners; again she frowned at the weight of her boat that lagged behind her sisters' while our youth cringed with guilt; again they fled first through the diamond forest glistening with prisms; again through the thick honeyed light of the gold forest and lastly through the ghostly glow of the silver forest, racing the dawn.

At last they reached the palace walls once more and slipped through the cold stone passage. Our youth realised with horror that he must overtake the fair dancers to be discovered asleep in their room, and he fumbled past. But as he passed the sixth sister, she trod on his cloak and it slipped clean off. And there he was, in his underwear before the twelve Princesses all crowded against each other in the narrow passage.

****

The forest wishes to keep its secrets. So when the sun rose pink and blue above the mountains, the three fairy forests were once more invisible. The sun rose higher and the pall of night slipped apace, racing back up the mountain while the pine trees donned their morning dress of purple and gold light.

The sun had nearly bathed the palace while the twelve Princesses held council over what was to be done with their goat herder.

"Kill him," said the second eldest.

"Nay sister, just take the branches and destroy them; no one will believe him," said another.

"We should hear his defence," decided the sixth sister.

Her twin sanctioned this and the other ten were brought to agree. And the goat herder confessed his meeting with the wizened wise woman in the stillest part of the forest while the sisters exchanged glances; poured forth his humble soul on the seeming unworthiness of those foreign Princes and begged mercy of the sisters.

"Leave me," he begged, "to return to my hillside and my old father. I will be ever content alone with the visions I have seen and enriched with the beauty of your secrets!"

The sisters conferred.

"We have a better idea," said the eldest.

****

The King's Court sat in State; the King on his throne with six daughters to his left, and six daughters to his right. The goat herder, now refreshed, was called upon to give his answer.

He told the forest's secrets. He explained first the silver forest and brought forth the shimmering bough as proof. He described the golden forest, then the diamond, holding up each bright branch to show them all. He described the lake and the cave, and finally the beautiful ball with its hours of joyous dancing that left the Princesses' shoes so spoilt.

The King congratulated him. He scowled at his daughters and growled under his breath that they would be punished for their disobedience. He granted the goat herder the Duchy, the amethysts, and the pick of his daughters. The goat herder expressed how he found the sixth daughter most captivating, but what was that to a Princess; and moreover, he would only accept the King's gifts at his daughters' consent.

Now this threw the King into a great rage. He railed at his daughters for bewitching the young man; for their wilful passion and their sordid peasant diversions. He was calling the guards to have them confined when the eldest Princess stood up.

"Too long have you oppressed us with your austerity and harshness father. Too long have you thwarted our pleasures and abused our heritage. Our mother your Queen died not, but returned to her own Kingdom in the forest. We are her changeling daughters all and we have been dancing in the forest these months with our own kin, to feast with our mother. And now, we take our rights."

The twelve Princesses surrounded the King and the eldest grasped a dagger from her belt sheath and slit his throat. In that moment, the three branches flew from the goat herder's hand and blossomed into three beautiful, tall trees as a glimmering bower protecting the Princesses and their goat herder at their feet.

A shout went up from the courtiers.

"The King is dead! Long live the Queen!"

****

Beneath the trees of this land are the smothered mountains. Cowslips and lady's bedstraw bloom so gold in the summer that children in the valley say they turn to pure gold at night. The river pours its falls down the mountain precipice and throws glittering diamond prisms on the trunks of trees. The forests open and green soft slopes grazing cattle emerge. The vines in this land bear the sweetest wines. Folk say this Kingdom is protected and blessed, and the joyful Queen who rules ordains many dances, pageants, and festivals for the holidays of her prosperous people. Older folk say warmly how their children enjoy much more dancing now than they themselves ever did.

The Queen's eleven sisters form the council of this land, and the sixth is married to a local boy who still tends his goats between Royal duties, and all are very happy. On the Queen's Jubilee day there is now the tradition of huge gold, silver and diamond trees set up on the green and all folk dance under them and mysterious, beautiful men and women come from the forest and dance with peasant and Princess alike. The young goat herder greets them warmly and shows his sons and daughters. He teaches them many things of this world and the other.

What of the old woman who advised our goat herder in the stillest part of the forest? She attends these annual celebrations in her gold gown, her limbs lithe and shimmering, and she kisses and blesses her daughters and her glowing grandchildren.

And she winks at the youth. She always liked a strong boy with spirit.

So long as he did as he was told.

What Grandma Knew About Magpies

I listen to the magpie flute. It sings like stream water dancing in this dry land. The plain spreads its carpets before me, bordered by blue hills stretching their backs up to scratch on a pale sky. Peridot eucalypts tremble in the wind on bone white legs that step between the grey boulders and dead trunks that look like silent kangaroos on the brown grassland.

Then the crimson of rosellas wounds the brown green with vibrance and emerald king parrots shuffle on the branches. I am relieved by colour. Over the years I have tired of monochrome. But this new sound of the magpie's voice will never tire me. I watch it stalk through the eucalyptus tinder with its white collar and black lipped beak – that long sharp beak grandma used to threaten would pluck out our eyes.

What did grandma know?

After she died, her stories about stealing magpies that stole my sister still live, and now I have come to the home of swooping magpies where they have never heard the children's rhyme to barter for her back.

Grandma was born in Australia and I came to find out what she knew. Why her frown creased at talk of witches' familiars. But she died before I could ask, leaving us only photographs of unknown little girls she used to teach in France and horrid stories about magpies bitter in my mouth.

But she never told us how beautiful their song was. This call like a flute trickling down from the branches is so ethereal against the English magpie chutter. It flicks new ripples with a tickling tongue I can't see and weeps of my loss. And my sister never heard it. I swallow the ache that has yawned in me since the day I stopped saying 'we;' since the day one English magpie sang for sorrow over me, alone. And now I am here to find a way to make the magpies give her back.

* * * *

I tried to lie down and wait to die. But I was made to get up – brave face – big girl – carry on, and the insult is that I did. Nothing is sacred. As I grew older, I lived the dull half-life of aches. As a child I was gouged out by the loss of half myself. As a woman I was lacerated by longings I could now name and list. I turned them over in my hands; lined them up on shelves in my empty home to look at.

Loss

Space Absence: the shape of the hole of her. How our arms and chins and shoulders could lock together, and we liked to put our hands on our narrow shoulders and see how close together they were. How our hands twined into finger plaits. The hovering gravity pulling, even if one turned away the weight was thick and safely there.

Future Absence: we used to talk about growing up and what we'd be like. That we would have a flat in Paris and gabble in French drinking wine in the kitchen. That we would explore mountains; swim in lakes and walk in forests. We did not know the forest dangers then.

Sharing Absence: endless repeated phrases whose origins we have forgotten from a game once played or a book read long ago. Knowing each other's every movement, every expression examined for weakness, always on guard with the comfort of a wordless hand press when one smelled the other's sadness coming on.

Talking Absence: events of life only became solid when we told them to each other; finished with and neatly put away. Forgetting to tell each other something made it unreal and illusory until words and ears gave it firm shape and pinned it down.

Silence Absence: running out of things to talk about. Looking out of the window. Closing eyes. Smiling.

The Worst One: Forgetting she is gone and turning to write in the cream pages of her face in my blue-eyed ink but there is nothing; she is not there; there is no diary for my heart now – it tears and rips afresh and I am rags again.

* * * *

I learned to do things on my own. I ate my meals staring at the window and walked the lanes and fields with myself. I slept alone and read books in great chairs stuffed with cushions so as not to feel cold absence. I grew up called 'her' instead of 'them,' got a job and somewhere to live. And from my kitchen, wineless and sisterless, I watched the magpies; biding my time until I flew on steel wings here.

In my new home by an empty creek, I watched the magpies for many days. I had learned now at least to make offerings and every morning I opened the kitchen door and threw down crumbs and pieces of cheese. I bought seed mix and scattered it on the wooden raised porch in the wattle and casuarina shade until the ground was flecked white with shit and my kitchen rang with magpie flutes. I fed the young ones, foolish and bold, like little girls who have not learned caution, and they stepped in through the threshold and piped their not-quite whistles brazenly. Their backs were dirty grey, but as winter drew on, they burnished ebony sharp and the white collar was like stiff French lace. They looked at me one morning with rubies for eyes – blood red – then built their nests above my porch.

Grandma was right. I watched from the window as the magpie swooping made me a hermit. The postman disdained the street and went around; I never had letters anyway. Magpies skimmed the air; beaks daubed with red gore and their songs in sinister minor. But I walked onto my porch every dawn with the golden wattle dancing fragrant and fed them seeds from my palms. Drinking pressed coffee, I stood in the blue morning where clouds cast pools of shadow on the great hill at the end small of the street where civilisation gave up and ran to grey and white bush. I listened to the bubbling of rosellas, the wailing of crows and the cockatoo raucous. I breathed in the soft herb scents of the forests and the magpies would sing to me, drive away evil and introduced their fledgling children.

Then one morning, in midsummer, I awoke to the roar of silence. I went outside and climbed up to look at the nest. It was empty. The magpie families had silenced the silver and gold of their voices and had flown away in the night.

* * * *

Winter is drier in this country. In my native land winter pours out of the sky and churns the fields and lanes to mud. Winter drips off the naked branches of trees and when you walk out, your face, your hair, your scarf, your boots are sodden. Here water is not frivolous and the grasses scratch in brown earth and the slender fingers of eucalyptus leaves are more silver than green. This morning, ice clutches the trees' fallen tinder and I lean over the porch railing with my coffee steam and fog breath mingling white and still.

A magpie drops and perches on the wooden beam. His red eyes stare at my blue and he cocks his head thoughtfully, patiently. He sings.

And I understand. I follow him into the forest.

* * * *

Up the dry hill between the starched white bones of trees, I follow the magpie. His beak drips spring blood on the wattle's yellow buds, his omen promise. At the summit, I come to a clearing strewn with gum nuts; hung with long slender-leafed garlands and here is the Magpie Queen. The Magpie grandmother with all her bloodthirsty children; warrior mothers who protect their flock's children viciously. They sing. These are the chicks I have fed, and they welcome me. I sit at the Magpie Mother's clawed feet.

She spreads her white cloak around her back and her black gown is long and sweeping. Her white lace collar is tall and regal and she greets me in her mournful song. She thanks me for my offerings to her children and asks me to name a gift.

I tell her. I tell her of a Magpie king who tricked me. A wicked white waistcoated black cloaked bird who stole my twin; who punished us for finding the seven secrets of the magpie court and left me one, sorrowing. I weep my tale and she draws her white cloak around my heaving solitude and holds me. Her red eyes bleed sadness on my white shoulder; her soft feathers comfort.

When she opens her beak to sing, it is the saddest flute I have ever heard and my heart cuts anew.

Magpies mate for life, but she was forsaken.

A cruel king holds her heart and my sister and if I will make a sacrifice, I will get them both. An eye for an eye. A sister for a heart.

I lie down before the Magpie Queen. Her red eyes still weep for me, but she is strong. I hold steady as she plucks out my blue eye with her sharp long beak and bids me take it to the Magpie king for a final offering. I stand up, half blind. My eye is now magpie red and I hold the sapphire in my hand. I leave the forest to the orchestra of magpies.

I go back to the forest of silver winter canopy and rough brown bark.

I go into the forest at night.

Through the dark, I walk holding up my sapphire eye for light. Through its diamond blue glow, I see my path with the light of the forest's secrets. The wind blows the leaves with the sound of water hissing over pebbles and its suspirations build to the chick and chutter of birds. I follow a crook in the path to a clearing and at last I have re-found the Magpie Court. Here is its amethyst throne; its pillars of pearl and emerald; its pile of shining treasure.

And here, barred by white and black feathers; grown not tall, but woman; is my sister.

The Magpie King screeches his laughter with his beak close to the socket of my eye. I hold up the sapphire. He shuffles back, his eyes glittering onyx with greed.

You can have it, I tell him, when you give her back.

The magpies scream and chuckle and press against me. I can see my sister over their corvid heads as they try to snatch the sapphire. Coughing feathers, I shuffle backwards, her gravity and weight pulling me like a magnet.

They will try to steal my sapphire and keep my sister. But this is what grandma knew, and I now know, magpies will not swoop when you fix them with your eye.

I hold the sapphire high up, carefully so my fingers don't obscure its sparkle. The magpies pause, hypnotised. I reach my sister's arms and we back away between the columns of trees. I kick against something hard as I shuffle away – a box crusted with rubies. My stumble overturns it, and out tumbles a magpie heart. My sister swoops to scoop it back into the box and tucks it under her arm. Our hearts are thundering, and our underarms and palms are damp from fear. Then with a great launch, we throw the sapphire into the cluster of magpies and run.

The sapphire hits the King in the eye. He is blinded as the court squawk and flap around him; the sapphire lodges tight and he screams in the blue agony.

An eye for eye, a heart for a sister.

Holding hands and heart, we run out of the forest.

C. E. Collins is a Morris dancing, shanty singing English teacher who writes. Her passion for mythology, folklore and nature is the inspiring force behind her work in which she creates a space for women's voices. Her prose and poetry have been published by presses and journals in the UK, US and Australia including Between These Shores Literary Annual, Not Very Quiet Journal, Scarlet Leaf Publishing House, Twist in Time Magazine, Animal Heart Press, Cephalopress, Sledgehammer Lit and Enchanted Conversation. Her non-fiction has featured on ABC Radio National and she has published many poetry reviews including in The Awakenings Review.

Rebecca Freeman's practice embraces paper-based techniques including printmaking, drawing and paper cutting. The art reflects her fascination with the immeasurable capacity for storytelling as a tool to entertain, teach, record, comfort and deceive. Drawing common themes and motifs from folk tales and contemporary literature she combines this transcriptive approach with original ideas and images drawn from her own experience and imagination. She won the Joseph Webb ARE Commemorative Award for an outstanding etcher under 35 in 2011 and has exhibited at the Mall Galleries, London.

****